Frustration taunted her. She'd hoped one visit to Covington Plantation would supply her with all the information she needed to find the young man.

How was she to know the place didn't even exist anymore?

Her conversation with Dale Covington raised more questions than it answered. She leaned back in her chair and gazed out the small curtained window. Orange and red leaves mingled with bronze and gold in a gorgeous crazy-quilt mosaic, a gentle reminder that no matter how ugly war's destruction, God had the power to make things beautiful again.

"What if some things can never be put back together? What if I have to go back to Harrisburg and tell Essie I couldn't find Wylie, or worse, what if he's dead?"

The familiar twinge of grief pierced her chest. Her goal of finding her father remained unspoken. No one but God knew of her intention to learn what had befallen him, and she knew the chance of finding him alive was almost zero. But if she could simply know for sure, perhaps the troubled dreams that invaded her sleep would come to an end.

CONNIE STEVENS

lives in north Georgia with her husband of over thirty-five years, John. She and John are active in a variety of capacities in their home church. One cantankerous kitty—misnamed Sweet Pea—allows them to live in *her* home. Some of Connie's favorite pastimes include reading, sewing, browsing antique shops, collecting teddy bears, and gardening. She also enjoys making quilts to send to the Cancer Treatment Center of America. Visit Connie's website and blog at www.conniestevenswrites.com.

Books by Connie Stevens

HEARTSONG PRESENTS

Harbinger of Healing

Connie Stevens

Heartsong Presents

To JoAnne Simmons, my first editor.
Thank you for letting God use you
to make my dreams come true.

A note from the Author:

*I love to hear from my readers! You may correspond with
me by writing:*

Connie Stevens
Author Relations
P.O. Box 9048
Buffalo, NY 14240-9048

ISBN-13: 978-0-373-48639-7

HARBINGER OF HEALING

This edition issued by special arrangement with Barbour Publishing,
Inc., 1810 Barbour Drive, Uhrichsville, Ohio, U.S.A.

Chapter 1

September 1870

Charity Galbraith choked back the retort dancing on her tongue with a garbled cough. Uncle Luther's opinions of her occupation and the station to which he believed all women were born grated on her nerves. Had she known a nonstop dissertation of his narrow-minded views would accompany her south, she'd never have entreated him to be her traveling escort.

She turned toward the train's grimy window and muttered under her breath, "Perhaps I should feign sleep." If she had to endure five more minutes of his diatribe, she'd surely throw the nearest loose object at him. Said object happened to be her thrice-read volume of *Jane Eyre*. No, she'd never treat the intrepid heroine of her favorite novel so shabbily. Perhaps the stale liverwurst sandwich her uncle had magnanimously bestowed on her would serve as a better projectile.

Two days of train travel with her pompous, cigar-puffing uncle frayed the threads of her poise dangerously thin. She returned her attention to her chaperone and sugared her tone. "It may make you feel better to know that my editor shares your opinion of women writers and therefore requires that I use a masculine pen name."

Uncle Luther's thick, black eyebrows bristled together like a fat caterpillar preparing for winter. "He does? Your articles don't bear your name?"

Pricks of irritation made her squirm, and she glanced at the novel in her lap. If female authors of fiction were now acceptable, why not of magazine articles? The upper crust of society made up the majority of the magazine's audience, and they apparently weren't ready to read the expressed viewpoint of current events from the female perspective. "The readership of *Keystone Magazine* thinks my articles are written by Charles Galbraith."

Speaking her father's name sent waves of sorrow through her. Major Charles Hampton Galbraith of the Federal army never returned home after the War of Southern Rebellion, and the ache to know what became of him still haunted her.

A *harrumph* met her ears, and she braced herself for more of Uncle Luther's unsolicited criticism.

"What would your father think of the unseemly usage of his name?"

Her eyes burned and she swallowed hard. "Even though most everyone in Harrisburg knew him as Hampton Galbraith, I use his first name in tribute to him."

He muttered something she couldn't quite hear over the monotonous rumble of the train wheels. She turned to squint out the soot-darkened window as the landscape lurched past. Where were they? Virginia? No, they changed trains in Washington some time ago, so surely they must be in North Carolina by now.

Had the train carried her enough miles from home to safely inform her uncle of her intentions? She twisted in her seat and found him buried behind his newspaper.

"I hope you'll be able to cancel the reservation for my room at the hotel in Atlanta."

The newspaper crumpled as Uncle Luther lowered it and sent her a scowl. "What are you talking about?"

A hint of defiance tiptoed through her, and she lifted her chin. "I don't plan to stay in Atlanta, Uncle. This trip is not only for the purpose of researching the series of articles for the magazine. I promised my friend back in Harrisburg, Essie Carver, that I'd search for her son."

"What? What kind of nonsense is this? Of course, you're staying in Atlanta under my protection. That Carver woman is a servant."

Ire flared in Charity's belly. "She's a businesswoman. She was born a slave and escaped that horrendous life. Now she makes her living as a seamstress."

Uncle Luther sniffed. "That hardly makes her a businesswoman. She's still a—"

"She's my friend." Charity interrupted him before he could use the despicable word. "You know how dangerous it is for a Negro woman to return to the South alone. Even though it's been six years since the war, Negroes aren't looked upon with favor in those states. Besides, she hasn't the money or the connections for such a search. Essie hasn't seen her son, Wylie, since he was sold to a neighboring plantation eleven years ago. He was only thirteen. She doesn't know if he's alive or dead."

"I still don't see why you must take it upon yourself. Why can't this Wylie initiate the search." He shook his head until his jowls flapped. "What about your family's reputation? What will people think of you going off to find this slave—"

"He's no longer a slave." Her fingers curled around the end of the armrest of the lumpy seat. "That's what my father—your brother—fought for. He believed nobody has the right to own another human being. Essie and Wylie are but two of the people for whom my father fought."

Uncle Luther grunted and snapped open his newspaper without another word. Grateful for the silence except for the clackety-clacking of the wheels rolling down the track, Charity allowed her thoughts to wander back to her last conversation with Essie. All the woman could tell her was the name of the plantation to which Wylie had been sold— Covington Plantation, near a town called Juniper Springs.

There was a third aspect to her journey, the purpose of which she'd shared with no one. Her research assignment for the magazine not only offered the opportunity to search for Essie's son, but also to pursue the desire of her heart for the past six years. She prayed for God's help in learning what had become of her father.

Her mother had kept the few letters they'd received from him in the drawer of the china cabinet, and the paper had grown yellowed and worn from the number of times Charity and her mother had taken them out and read them. The last word from the war department indicated Father had been wounded and taken prisoner at a battle in northern Georgia—some place called Pickett's Mill. She and her mother had been left to wait and wonder. Mama had taken her broken heart to her grave, but Charity still longed to know the truth.

Growling snores emerged from behind Uncle Luther's newspaper. Charity set aside her book and rose, stretching her stiff legs. She gingerly stepped past her uncle's sprawled out form and held on to the corners of the seat backs to keep her balance as the train lurched along, carrying her deeper into the Southern countryside. Making her way toward the back of the railcar, she hailed the conductor.

"Sir? Can you tell me how much longer it will be before we arrive in Atlanta?"

The plump, rosy-cheeked man peered at her over the top of his lopsided spectacles. "This here train don't go to Atlanta, miss. It goes on to Savannah. You'll be changin' trains and headin' westbound at Augusta. We're scheduled to arrive in Augusta at nine forty-five tomorrow mornin'."

"I see." She glanced back at her uncle whose snores could be heard all the way back to where she stood conversing with the conductor. "Do you happen to have the westbound schedule?"

He beamed and proudly pulled a small black booklet from his jacket pocket. "Of course. Let's see." He licked his thumb and pushed back a couple of pages. "Here it is. Westbound train leaves Augusta at eleven ten in the mornin', and it stops to take on water at Madison. It'll get you into Atlanta at six fifteen tomorrow evenin'."

"Is there a northbound train from Madison?"

"Uh-huh. Train runs between Madison and Athens every day."

She thanked the man and returned to her seat, a plan formulating in her head.

Charity rummaged around in her satchel for her comb. There wasn't anything she could do with her rumpled, travel-disheveled clothing, but at least she could tidy her hair. Uncle Luther and some other men had moved to the smoking car to discuss business over brandy and cigars, leaving Charity to watch out the window for the sign indicating they were coming into Madison. The westbound train was shorter than the southbound and didn't haul as many freight cars, thus allowing the train to make better time.

The whistle sounded and the brakes squealed, slowing the train around a bend in the tracks.

"Madison. Madison, Georgia, ladies and gentlemen." The conductor made his way through the car calling out the information. "We'll stop here for about fifteen minutes, so don't go far."

"Excuse me, sir." Charity reached out and touched the man's elbow.

"Yes, miss?"

"I'll be disembarking the train at Madison. Could you please see that my trunk is taken off the baggage car?" She handed him her claim stub.

This conductor wasn't as pleasant as the one from the southbound train. He glanced at the stub and sent her a surly scowl. "Yer ticket goes through to Atlanta, don't it?"

"Yes, it does, but my plans have changed. Please remove my trunk."

He grumbled but headed toward the back of the railcar. Charity picked up her satchel and left the note she'd penned explaining her departure to Uncle Luther on the empty seat. Gathering her skirts about her, she quickly stepped toward the door, hoping she'd not encounter her uncle. Judging by the boisterous laughter coming from the smoking car, the men were well into the bottle of brandy.

Charity hurried across the platform to the ticket window. "One-way ticket to Athens, please." She dug in her reticule for her coin purse. "Might I be able to hire a carriage in Athens to take me to the town of Juniper Springs?"

The clerk assured her carriages were available at a price. A porter thumped her trunk down on the platform. Minutes later, the train hissed and belched steam. The whistle sounded and the behemoth groaned, rolling westward toward Atlanta and leaving Charity standing in a swirling cloud of soot and dust.

Dale Covington rolled his head from side to side to unkink the tightened muscles in his neck, and once more thanked God for the job he had at the sawmill. It had taken him some time to develop the muscular arms and calloused hands required for the manual labor—work he'd never known before the war. It was a good thing his father couldn't see him now.

Dale limped across the bridge that led to the town of Juniper Springs, but he still had work to do before returning to the small house he rented from Simon Pembroke, the Yankee who moved to Georgia after the war and built the sawmill. How many times had Dale come to the end of a long day and thought about the opulent home he'd once occupied with his parents and later with his wife?

The old wound in his leg hampered his progress as his hitched gait carried him toward the general store and his second job. Clyde Sawyer, the man who ran the mercantile, always had odd jobs for Dale to do and deliveries for him to make. The extra job enabled Dale to add a few more dollars a month to his savings. One day he'd be a landowner again. He set aside his weariness and pushed open the back door of the store.

"Clyde?"

A stocky man with wisps of gray hair around his ears stepped through the curtained doorway and wiped perspiration off his balding head with the corner of his denim apron. "Afternoon, Dale. There's a couple of orders on the clipboard to be delivered, and those crates by the door gotta be unpacked. Why don't you take a sit-down first? You look like you could use it."

Dale shook his head. "If it's all right with you, I'll unpack the new stock first and deliver those orders on my way home."

"Fine with me. Oh, my Sweet Pea made some cookies this mornin'. Said to make sure to save you some." Clyde pointed to a cloth-covered basket. "They're under that blue-checked napkin. Help yourself."

"Thanks. And tell Betsy I said thank you to her, too."

Clyde bobbed his head and returned to the front of the store, whistling as he went. Dale envied Clyde. The man had always led a simple, hardworking life. He'd never known wealth and therefore didn't miss it. He had a wife he adored who loved him in return, and by all appearances he seemed completely content with his life. How much easier would it be to face each day without regrets, disappointments, and grief?

Dale heaved a sigh and munched on a cinnamon-crusted cookie while he pried open the heavy crates. Ammunition and gun-cleaning supplies filled one crate, sewing supplies and button hooks in another. Three more contained canning jars and foodstuffs. Bolts of new cloth were stacked atop the last crate.

By the time he got everything unpacked, checked off the bills of lading, and ready for Clyde to stock the following morning, the sun hovered just above Yonah Mountain to the west. Dale stacked the two crates he'd set aside for the Juniper Springs Hotel and carried them two doors down, entering through the side door by way of the alley. Using the servants' entrance galled him at the beginning, but now he shrugged it off and set the crates down. The head housekeeper signed for them, and Dale made his way back to the mercantile to pick up the crate destined for the boardinghouse. As soon as he dropped off this order, he could head to his little cottage and solitary supper.

He limped across the street with the boardinghouse order and went around to the kitchen door. Amiable chatter reached his ears when he knocked on the back door. Hannah Sparrow, the widow who ran the boardinghouse, greeted him.

"Come in, Dale." She held the door open for him.

"Thank you, Mrs. Sparrow."

She plunked her hands on her hips. "When are you going to call me Hannah like everyone else?" Without waiting for a reply, she fluttered her fingers. "Excuse me. I must see to my new boarder." She left Dale to take the grocery items out of the wooden box and lay them on the worktable, and while he did so, he could hear her making introductions in the dining room.

"Everyone, this is Miss Charity Galbraith. She's a reporter with *Keystone Magazine*."

Dale peered through the crack in the door to get a look at the newcomer. An attractive, dark-haired woman in a maroon skirt and white shirtwaist stood beside Mrs. Sparrow. A collection of greetings blended in disharmony as Mrs. Sparrow introduced Miss Galbraith to everyone seated at the table.

"This is Frances Hyatt. She's our dressmaker. Miles Flint there is the sheriff in our county. Polly Ferguson and her daughter, Margaret, run the bakery down the street. Elden Hardy is a wheelwright, and he's from West Virginia. Arch Wheeler works at the land office, and across from him is Tate Ridley. Tate works at the sawmill."

Miss Galbraith greeted each person in turn, and her northern accent rasped across Dale's ears like sandpaper. The reporter was a Yankee—if he didn't miss his guess, she was from Pennsylvania.

Tate Ridley spoke up. "What sort o' articles you plannin'

on writin' 'bout our town, Miss Galbraith?" Dale detected the familiar belligerent tone in Tate's voice.

"*Keystone* has assigned a series of articles to me on the Reconstruction. I'm here to research and document the progress of putting our country back together after the war."

Dale gritted his teeth. Reconstruction, indeed. How many times did he have to be reminded of all he'd lost until the pain finally dulled? For the thousandth time he wondered if his decision to stay in Juniper Springs after the war was prudent. There were any number of places he could have started over, but the ugly memories would have dogged his steps no matter where he'd gone.

Why would a woman reporter travel to Georgia alone? He'd seen more northern carpetbaggers than he cared to count, but she certainly didn't look like someone who was here to snatch up cheap land or make money on the misery of others. He didn't wait to hear any more.

Dale let himself out the back door and headed down the now-darkened street toward his small rented house. There was a crisp coolness to the air—an onset of autumn? Or perhaps the chill that permeated his bones was generated by the voice of the Yankee woman at the boardinghouse.

Chapter 2

Dale opened one eye. An irritatingly cheerful bird perched in the maple tree outside his window proclaiming the dawn of the Lord's Day. After tossing and turning most of the night, his mind filled with images from the war and its aftermath, Dale scowled at the morning light streaming into the room. Sunday morning, the only day he didn't have to work. He rolled over, turning his back to the window, and pulled the pillow over his head. But despite squeezing his eyes closed and pressing the pillow to his ear, he couldn't block out the feathered herald's insistence that he arise and dress for church.

Stupid bird.

He swung his feet over the side of the bed and raked his fingers through his hair. Yawning and stretching, he exited the small bed chamber and shuffled across the main room to see if any live coals remained in the stove. No welcoming red pinpoints glowed from within. Grumbling, he assembled a handful of kindling and wood chips, stuffing them into the firebox. He struck a match and dropped it in among the dry tinder, watching it catch and burn.

"I need a cup of coffee." He grabbed the coffeepot and shook it hopefully, but there was no happy gurgling. Lack of sleep fueled his surly disposition as he shoveled several spoonfuls of grounds into the pot and ladled water over it. While he waited for the pot to boil, he sat at the small, shabby table with the Bible Pastor Shuford gave him. No doubt the preacher would ask him if he'd been reading it. He opened the Book where the scrap of paper marked his place and began reading.

"Psalm thirteen. 'How long wilt thou forget me, O Lord? For ever? How long wilt thou hide thy face from me?' " He leaned back and stared at the words. How did the writer of the psalm know exactly how Dale felt? The verse echoed through his hollow being, rattling the bitter crust around his heart. He looked heavenward and pointed to the pages, as though God were unaware of what it said.

"Why God? The psalmist, David, was a godly man and this says You turned Your back on him. He only asked how long, but I'm asking why. Why was my world devastated? Why did You take everything from me?" The well-kept chronicle Dale hid in his heart emerged, and he mentally went down the list of everything he'd lost.

His old war wounds—the one in his side as well as his leg—began to ache in unison along with the canker in his spirit. He rubbed his hand over the scar on his left side under his ribs.

"God, I really do want to live for You, but every time I take a step toward You, my feet slip out from under me and I'm back where I started. I don't want to live in the pit of despair, but I don't know how to climb out."

The quiet whisper of heaven's voice nudged him to keep

reading. He returned to the psalm and found an affinity with the writer in the next verses. "Sorrow in my heart... mine enemy be exalted over me..."

But the last two verses of the short psalm weren't what he expected. "But I have trusted in thy mercy; my heart shall rejoice in thy salvation. I will sing unto the Lord, because he hath dealt bountifully with me."

He shook his head. "Bountifully? How is losing everything meaningful to a man considered bountiful?"

Recurring nightmares from the war weren't the only thing that kept slumber at bay last night. That Yankee woman he'd seen at the boardinghouse yesterday lingered in his thoughts. Her winsome smile charmed him until she spoke. The sound of her Northern accent mocked him with the reminder of all that the war had stolen from him.

How ridiculous. It was unfair to blame Miss Galbraith for his losses by virtue of her birthplace. She was not the one who burned his home, nor did she fire the rifle that inflicted his wounds. Still, did she not represent the ones who did?

Hisshhhh. The coffeepot boiled over. Dale jumped up and limped over to the stove, grabbing a rag to mop up the mess. He muttered his annoyance and gazed through the open door that separated the tiny bedroom from the main living space. The rumpled bedcovers and lumpy mattress tick called to him. Falling under the alluring spell of his pillow seemed more prudent than shaving and dressing for church, but Pastor Shuford would no doubt come knocking on his door later this afternoon if he didn't go. He sighed and went to fetch his razor.

The Sunday service was already underway when Dale hop-stepped up the front stairs of the church. The congregation's fine voice filled the early-autumn morning, much like the mockingbird that had awakened him. Their song gilded the air with praise, but Dale's grumpiness had accompanied him to church. He slipped in the door and found a place near the back, scowling at the toes of his boots. Maybe he wouldn't have to fellowship with anyone if he sat in the back.

From his vantage point, he could study the backs of everyone's heads and noted his boss, Simon Pembroke, sat directly in front of him. His gaze moved down the row, and he picked out Doctor Greenway and the Sawyers. Across the aisle, his sister, Auralie, her husband, Colton, and their two children sat sharing a Bible. Dale gritted his teeth and pulled his gaze away. When Colton fought with the Yankees, Dale had told Auralie she was no longer his sister.

He directed his vision straight ahead. Five rows ahead of him, a woman with dark walnut hair pinned up under a ridiculous purple hat sat beside Hannah Sparrow.

Pastor Shuford's voice filled the room as he announced his text for the morning. Dale paid little attention to the reference, but when the preacher began relating the biblical account of Peter inquiring of Jesus how many times he must forgive, Dale jerked his focus to the pulpit. He narrowed his eyes at the pastor, certain the clergyman spoke directly to him. After all, how many others in the congregation struggled with unwillingness to forgive those who had wronged them? If he rose to leave, everyone would notice his halting gait heading for the door, so he sat still and tried not to listen.

His gaze kept returning to the woman in the purple hat, and when she turned her head momentarily, Dale realized it was Miss Galbraith. How ironic, or appropriate, that the woman whose presence had stirred his rancor and interrupted his sleep, who represented those he refused to forgive, sat not fifteen feet in front of him.

* * *

Charity tucked her lower lip between her teeth to keep from standing up and demanding the preacher stop trampling on her toes. If there was a topic to which she did not wish to listen, it was God's instruction to forgive. How dare this minister suggest it was her obligation to forgive the people who had taken her father from her?

She turned to the scripture the preacher indicated with the intention of checking to see if he had taken it out of context and twisted its meaning. Matthew chapter eighteen, beginning in verse twenty-one. She read all the way through to verse thirty-five searching for the smallest detail to which she could point and disagree. But the plain truth of Christ's example lay across the pages in black and white. The thought of graciously granting forgiveness to those who didn't deserve it set her teeth on edge.

It stood to reason many Southerners harbored resentment since they lost the war, but hearing such a message preached in a Southern church indeed surprised her. Charity sent a surreptitious glance around the room, looking for people who appeared as offended as she at the minister's audacity. There were some who scowled or looked away from the man in the pulpit, but many nodded their heads or murmured "amen."

The pastor drew the congregation's attention to Luke chapter six. "In verse thirty-seven, Jesus tells us not to judge so we will not be judged, nor condemn others so we will not be condemned. Our Lord adds that if we expect to be forgiven, we must learn to forgive." The man stepped to the side of the pulpit, reaching out an upturned palm, beseeching the listeners. "Don't allow the spirit of unforgiveness to devour you. Your refusal to forgive another doesn't hurt that person nearly as much as it hurts you."

In the two days she'd been in Juniper Springs, the sound

of Southern twang had grated on her ears, and this preacher was no different. But it wasn't the sound of his voice as much as the meaning of his words that offended her. How could she do what he advocated? Some days her anger was the only thing that fueled her motivation to go on. Clinging to malice made her strong. Charity drew the shutters of her heart closed and refused entry to the remainder of the sermon.

She'd begged her editor to let her write the series of articles on Reconstruction. The South started the fight, demanding their right to use slaves or their very way of life would be destroyed. Of course there were casualties inflicted in the South, but after all, they were the ones who rebelled and seceded. Soldiers like her father were defending their sovereign nation. Besides, the very idea of slavery nauseated her. The South's insistence that their agriculture industry would suffer without slave labor was preposterous, and she intended to use her pen as a sword to carve indelible words to that effect.

The latest news from the South had made the headlines only a few weeks before she boarded the train to travel to Georgia. According to the *Harrisburg Gazette*, Georgia was finally readmitted to the Union after five years of refusing to comply with Federal orders. It wasn't until last February that the Georgia legislature finally ratified the fourteenth and fifteenth amendments, and the newspaper said it happened only at the point of military bayonets. Even now Federal troops still occupied McPherson Barracks in Atlanta to ensure no more lapses in compliance. Charity sniffed. Didn't that justify her feelings and prove her point?

Charity folded her arms. Nobody—not this preacher or anyone else—would convince her to extend unmerited forgiveness to people who had wronged so many.

She barely realized the rest of the congregation stood

until they began to sing, "O, for a closer walk with God, a calm and heavenly frame; a light to shine upon the road, that leads me to the Lamb."

She rose quickly and added her voice to the hymn, hoping no one noticed her lack of attention. When the singing faded away, the minister closed in prayer and bid everyone a blessed Sabbath. Charity picked up her Bible and reticule, and Hannah Sparrow beckoned a few parishioners over to introduce them.

More Southern accents.

She managed to smile and shake hands with each one; then her gaze collided with that of a young man standing near the back talking to the pastor. He stared at her for only a moment, his expression an odd mix of fascination and distrust. After a few seconds he turned back to his discussion with the pastor, but Charity studied his profile from across the room. She'd seen him before. That haunted look in his eyes jogged her memory. Of course—the man she saw through the kitchen door at the boardinghouse yesterday evening. She thought at first he worked there, but she didn't see him again until now. A darkness clung to him, nothing sinister, but somber and brooding, like he'd known great pain.

The preacher clapped him on the shoulder and turned to greet other worshipers. The young man with the moody eyes sent another quick look her way and caught her watching him. She stifled a gasp and turned to speak to Hannah Sparrow.

"Please excuse me, Mrs. Sparrow. I'd like to speak to the preacher."

"Wasn't this morning's message wonderful? I'm sure you'll enjoy meeting him," her landlady bubbled.

Charity didn't bother to explain that her interest in speaking with the man wasn't to discuss today's sermon.

As the pastor of the church, he likely knew everyone in town, and Charity hoped he could supply her with some information. When she made her way toward the pastor, the man she'd seen at the boardinghouse had already taken his leave, and Charity's curiosity remained unsatisfied.

Mrs. Sparrow took Charity's hand. "Pastor Shuford, I'd like you to meet my newest boarder, Miss Charity Galbraith. She is a reporter with *Keystone Magazine*."

The pastor shook her hand and gave her a warm smile. "I hope you'll be with us for a good long visit, Miss Galbraith."

"Thank you, Reverend. I hope to stay for as long as it takes to research the information I need."

Pastor Shuford smiled and nodded. "If I can be of any help, please let me know."

Exactly what Charity hoped he'd say. "As a matter of fact, I'd like to visit Covington Plantation. Perhaps you could direct me."

A saddened expression drooped the man's smile. "I'm afraid there is no more Covington Plantation. It was burned during the war. Scavengers."

"Oh dear." Charity bit her lip. "I hoped to speak with someone from the Covington family. You see, I'm trying to locate a former slave who worked there."

"A former slave?"

"Yes. His name is Wylie, and his mother is my friend. She's not seen or heard from him for eleven years. I'd like to find him for her."

The pastor sent a stealthy glance around them, and then leaned in and lowered his voice. "That sounds like a fine Christian act, and I pray God's safety for you as you search. Not everyone in these parts will appreciate such a mission. Unfortunately, Covington Plantation no longer exists, but you can speak to Dale Covington."

"I'd very much like to do that. Where might I find him?"

The pastor stepped to the open door of the church and pointed. "That's him, the man in the dark brown coat."

Charity looked at the man to whom the pastor pointed. The brooding man with the hollow look in his eyes limped across the street away from the church.

"He was wounded in the war." Pastor Shuford's voice, hushed and pensive, left Charity to wonder about the extent of Mr. Covington's wounds.

A dozen other questions crowded her mind as well. The Covingtons were obviously a wealthy family at one time if they owned a plantation and slaves. Curiosity needled her. Whatever was a man like that doing in the boarding-house kitchen?

"Miss Galbraith, I feel I must tell you, Dale Covington probably won't be very receptive to your inquiries."

She turned to look at the pastor. "Why? Is he ashamed of having kept slaves?"

Pastor Shuford gave an almost imperceptible shake of his head. "Sometimes a man's wounds go deeper than his flesh."

She pondered the minister's peculiar reply for a moment. "Could you direct me to his place of residence?"

"It wouldn't be proper for you to visit him at his home. He lives alone. I hope you understand." Pastor Shuford gave her a fatherly smile. "But he works at the sawmill across the creek." He pointed toward the left. "Go past the boardinghouse and the post office. The road curves and you'll see a bridge. You can find him there most days. After he finishes at the mill, he works for Clyde Sawyer at the general store. He helps out in the back, makes deliveries, things like that."

So he'd been delivering Mrs. Sparrow's groceries last evening. Imagine that, a rich man like Covington working in a sawmill and delivering groceries. She supposed she should feel sympathy for him, but instead, an element of smug gratification settled in her stomach.

"Across the creek, you say?" She leaned to peer in the direction the pastor had pointed. "Thank you, Pastor. I'll pay Mr. Covington a visit at the sawmill."

Chapter 3

Dale hurried into the bakery on his way to the sawmill. Despite living alone for six years, he'd still not gotten used to making his own breakfast. Polly Ferguson always had some tempting offerings to satisfy him.

Polly's daughter, Margaret, greeted him. "Good morning, Dale. What can I get for you today?"

Dale peered over the counter to the baked goods lined up on racks behind her. "By any chance did you and your mother make those apple things this morning?"

Margaret's pleasant personality and culinary skills might have been enough to lure some men, but Dale wasn't hunting. Besides, the woman was a few years older than he, and plain-looking with her mousy hair pulled back in a tight bun. Her crooked teeth showed when she smiled.

"You mean the cinnamon apple scones? Yes, we made them. How many would you like?"

One fat scone would keep him going this morning. He'd

tried buying an extra one once, thinking he could eat it the following morning, thus saving himself a trip to the bakery. But by the second day the scone was so dry, it was like trying to swallow thatch.

"Just one."

Margaret wrapped a scone in paper and handed it to him with a demure smile. "I gave you the biggest one. Anything else?"

Dale had the distinct impression she was flirting. "No, thank you." He handed over a dime and took his wrapped breakfast.

"See you tomorrow, Dale?"

He hesitated on his way out the door. "Uh, maybe." As he exited, he nearly collided with Pastor Shuford.

"Morning, Pastor." He held up the scone. "Join me for breakfast?"

The preacher chuckled. "No, my wife keeps me supplied with all the baked goods I can eat. Actually, I saw you walking this way and thought I might accompany you to the sawmill if you don't mind."

Dale slid the scone into his pocket and glanced sideways at the preacher. "You thinking on buying some lumber, or is there another purpose to your early morning stroll?"

The older man smiled. "I confess I just wanted to talk to you. Let's walk so you aren't late for work."

The two set out in the direction of the sawmill. Dale noticed the pastor shortened his stride to accommodate Dale's hitched gait.

Pastor Shuford sucked in a noisy breath. "I love the smell of autumn."

Certainly the man didn't wish to discuss the changing seasons.

"I was talking with your sister and brother-in-law yesterday after church. Auralie and Colton said they haven't seen much of you."

"I've been busy." The ten-minute walk didn't afford much time for chatting. "What's really on your mind, Pastor?"

The pastor smiled. "I wondered if you'd given much thought to yesterday's sermon."

Dale drew in a stiff breath. He could have predicted this conversation. "Not too much. You know it's still hard for me to think about that. Everything you said is probably true, but I don't see why I should forgive people who burned my home, stole my land, and"—he gritted his teeth—"took Gwendolyn and—" Tightness took up residence in his throat.

Pastor Shuford's voice gentled. "Dale, you aren't the only one who lost someone in the war."

Dale halted and jerked around to face the preacher. "Maybe not, but when soldiers go off to fight, the ones left at home know there is a possibility they won't come back. After months of fighting and trying to heal from wounds, I came home expecting to find my loved ones waiting for me." He shook his head and continued toward the mill, his annoying shuffle-step impeding his determination to end this conversation and get to work.

The pastor fell in beside him. "Dale, have you ever noticed how your limp gets worse when you get angry about the war?"

Dale stopped so fast he almost pitched forward. He spun with an indignant retort on his tongue, ready to demand to know why the pastor would say something so cruel. But the preacher's expression was anything but cruel. Kindness and compassion deepened the lines around his eyes, defusing Dale's irritation.

"Dale." Pastor Shuford laid his hand on Dale's shoulder. The preacher's eyes glistened. "I fear the bullet that injured your leg did less damage than the resentment and animosity you nurture. Don't you see, son? Your old wound has been trying to heal for six years, but your bitterness is making you a cripple."

Pastor Shuford's words, spoken with such tenderness, punched Dale in the gut and robbed his breath. He braced himself with his good leg so he wouldn't stagger. No other person on the face of the earth could get away with saying such a thing to him. But even under the onslaught of pain the preacher's words brought, Dale knew the man well enough to realize he'd spoken in love.

He stared at his friend, watching the moisture gather in his eyes. The pastor squeezed Dale's shoulder before stepping back and dropping his hand.

"I better let you get on to work."

Dale nodded mutely, but didn't move.

"Son, you know I'm praying for you."

Dale somehow found the will to make his muscles work again. He nodded. "Yes, sir. I know."

He walked the remainder of the distance to the mill alone, but the preacher's words accompanied his every step. The morning mist still hung in the air as Dale studied his own impaired stride. Did his limp really worsen when he thought about the war?

Smoke curled from the tin chimney in the sawmill office. Simon Pembroke already had the fire in the potbellied stove going. Dale hitched his way up the dozen steps to the door that bore a sign, Pembroke Sawmill—Office. When he stepped inside, his boss looked up from the desk.

"You all right, Dale? You look a little peaked."

Dale gritted his teeth and worked his jaw. Pembroke's Northern accent always set him on edge, but even more so this morning. The man had arrived in Juniper Springs from Massachusetts the year after the war ended, bought up land cheap, and built the sawmill. It had galled Dale at first to work for a Yankee, but Pembroke paid a fair wage.

He sucked in a breath through his clamped teeth. "Yes, sir, just fine." He pulled the clipboard from its peg, but before he left the office to start on the day's first work order, he dug in his pocket and pulled out a few folded bills. He held them out to Pembroke. "October's rent for the house."

Pembroke frowned. "This isn't due till next week."

"I know." Dale laid the money on the desk and stepped out the door.

Charity walked resolutely down the street, past the post office, to the bend in the road. The bridge appeared on the left, just as the pastor said. She lifted her chin and straightened her shoulders, marching over the bridge. The sawmill was tucked into the rocks beside the creek so the swiftest running water turned the huge wheel. The noise from the mill drowned out the thumping of her heart in her ears. She paused at the end of the bridge.

Anticipation of speaking with Mr. Covington had her nerves tumbling, though she couldn't guess why. Arrogant, self-important people had never bothered her in the past. But something about this man intrigued her. He'd once been an influential man of means, but the outcome of the war had stripped him of his wealth. No doubt his circumstances would steer his reactions to her questions.

A set of stairs on one side of the large frame building led to a door with a sign declaring it to be the office. She pulled in a deep breath to strengthen her fortitude and proceeded toward the stairs. As she placed her foot on the first step, she saw him.

Mr. Covington, his back bent to his task and his sleeves rolled to his elbows, stacked lumber in the back of a wagon.

She watched him for a moment. Unsure of what she expected to see, an element of surprise raised her eyebrows as she observed the intensity and zeal with which he performed his job. He appeared different today, other than the fact he wore work clothes instead of his Sunday best. He gripped each board and maneuvered it smoothly into a neat stack with ease. That was it. His limp wasn't as noticeable today.

He straightened and reached for a canteen that hung from the side of the wagon. Just as he started to take a drink he caught sight of her and halted midmotion. He lowered the vessel slowly, his steely gaze fixed on her.

"Can I help you find something?"

Charity had an eerie feeling that he considered her an intruder. "Mr. Covington?"

He set the canteen aside. "That's right."

She pasted the most professional expression she could muster on her face and approached him. He stiffened visibly. Charity decided if he'd been a cat, he might have arched his back and hissed. She extended her hand.

"I'm Charity Galbraith."

His hooded eyes and the sullen twist to his mouth sent a chill through her, not from fear, but anticipation. What hovered behind those eyes?

He took her hand for a brief moment, but dropped it like it had burned him. "Miss Galbraith." There may as well have been a No Trespassing sign staked in front of him. This wasn't going to be easy.

"I wonder if you might have time to talk."

His dark eyes didn't blink. "I'm working."

"Yes, I can see that, but I promise I won't take up much of your time."

Several long seconds ticked by, and she thought he was going to tell her to leave, but he didn't. Instead, he gestured to a low stone wall on the side of the building beside the creek. He snagged the canteen and carried it with him.

When they were seated, he took the cap off the canteen and gave her an apologetic look. "Sorry, this is all I have to offer in the way of refreshment."

She waved her hand. "No, thank you, but you go ahead."

He took several gulps. "What is this about?"

Charity took a deep breath. "I have a friend in Pennsylvania. Her name is Essie Carver. She hasn't seen or heard from her son in eleven years. She's not even sure if he's alive."

Puzzlement etched its mark across his brow. "What does that have to do with me?"

"Essie's son's name is Wylie." She paused, searching his face for some flicker of recognition, but none appeared. "Wylie was a slave. He was sold to Covington Plantation in 1859 at age thirteen. That's the last she ever saw of him. I hope you can tell me where Wylie is now."

Distress lines between his eyes gave Mr. Covington a prematurely aged appearance. He rose and paced for a moment, as if unconscious of his limp. When he spoke, the painfulness of the topic was evidenced in his tone.

"I'm sorry, Miss Galbraith. Covington Plantation utilized over four hundred slaves. The only ones I knew by name were the house slaves and the ones who worked in the stables taking care of the horses and carriages." He glanced awkwardly at his crippled leg, hobbled slowly back to the stone wall, and sat, the limp more noticeable now than when he had been working.

"Records were kept, of course, but—" The muscles in his neck twitched as he swallowed. Was he trying to compose himself? "There was a fire. The records were destroyed along with…everything else." He rubbed his side with a slow, methodical motion. "It may seem inhumane to keep such a large number of slaves without knowing their names. When my father was alive, he and I frequently disagreed on the care of the slaves. I tried to tell him that treating them with brutality was unnecessary, but he insisted on leaving that up to the overseers." He looked across the lumberyard as if he was searching for the manor house in which he'd lived. "One of the things we disagreed on was splitting up family members. My father did not regard the slaves as having families. To him they were chattel."

Charity shook her head. "Are you telling me that a thirteen-year-old child came to work on your plantation and you were not aware of him?"

He rubbed his hand across his forehead. "Not if he was bought as a field slave." He turned to look at her. The moodiness in his eyes wavered. "I don't expect you to understand how it was."

Charity swallowed hard, trying to control her temper. How it was? How did he think it was for a child to be separated from his mother and for his mother to never know what happened to him?

"You're right, I don't understand."

He stood again and turned away from her with his hands clasped behind his back. "I was away much of the time. In the year or so before the war, I worked on some special projects for my father and out of necessity was away from the plantation for short periods. After—"

Though his back was to her, a visible shudder rippled through him, as though he bit off the words and spit them out.

"When the war started, I was commissioned and, of course, was away from home for much longer periods of time. When I returned home after the war, every—" He paused and sighed. "Everything...and everyone...was gone." He turned back to face her. "I sincerely wish I could help you find this Wylie. And I wish—I wish I'd known his name when he belonged to Covington Plantation."

Charity sat in silence, uncertain if she should feel pity or outrage toward this man. This conversation did not go as she expected. She'd come to the sawmill fully prepared to dislike Dale Covington. Her wavering emotions unsettled her, like a child walking atop a fence with arms held out to her sides for balance. She'd always held indecisive people in disdain. Now she was the object of her own scorn, the very attitude she'd reserved for Dale Covington.

"I really must get back to work." Mr. Covington fastened the top back onto the canteen.

Charity rose from her seat. "Thank you for your time, Mr. Covington. I suppose I'll have to look elsewhere for Wylie."

"You still intend to keep looking?" His question sounded more like a challenge.

"Of course." Did the man not understand what it meant to persevere? "I promised his mother."

Long after Miss Galbraith had taken her leave, Dale listened to their conversation echo in his mind. A cold sweat popped out on his forehead as the memories tore through him. His stomach tightened, and his leg ached. The picture he'd tried a thousand times to erase from his mind emerged again.

His uniform in tatters, a crutch under one arm, and sinking dread in his belly, he hobbled up the road toward home. Fear accosted him when he saw the great, ornate wrought-iron gates of Covington Plantation hanging askew from the posts. Grass grew down the lane that led to the manor house, and the once-beautiful grounds screamed out for someone to care for them once again.

He smelled it before he saw it. Although slight, the distinctive stench of stale smoke lingered in the air as though it didn't know where else to go. His first sighting of the burned-out ruins of the house nearly brought him to his knees, but that's not what ripped his heart from his chest.

Dale shook his head to rid himself of the memory—the scene he knew would invade his dreams again—and another took its place.

The black face bent over him, wrapping a rag around his leg and offering him a drink. The stranger removed his own shirt and used it to bind the wound in Dale's side. While rifle fire and artillery still roared, the black man whose name Dale did not know lifted him in his work-hardened arms and carried him to safety. For two days, the black man—obviously a slave sent to fight in his master's stead—cared for him until they reached a regiment that had a doctor.

"I wish I'd known his name."

Chapter 4

Charity propped her elbow on the small desk in the corner of her room at the boardinghouse and leaned her chin in her cupped palm. She'd composed a short letter to Uncle Luther, letting him know she was fine, staying in a respectable boardinghouse, and he needn't worry about her.

"*Pfft*. More likely he's glad to be rid of me." She addressed the envelope to her uncle, in care of the Kimball Hotel in Atlanta. Uncle Luther had made certain she'd known the Kimball was the finest hotel in the city, boasting of steam heat and elevators. She smirked at her uncle's pomposity.

Her second letter lay half-finished in front of her. She knew her editor at the magazine waited for a tentative list of interviews and useful research she'd gleaned. Convincing Mr. Peabody to give her this assignment wasn't easy. She couldn't disappoint him. She'd been in Juniper Springs for almost a week and most of her time had been spent simply observing and listening. She crumpled the paper into a ball.

"And trying to find Wylie." Frustration taunted her. She'd hoped one visit to Covington Plantation would supply her with all the information she needed to find the young man. How was she to know the place didn't even exist anymore?

Her conversation with Dale Covington raised more questions than it answered. She leaned back in her chair and gazed out the small curtained window. Orange and red leaves mingled with bronze and gold in a gorgeous crazy-quilt mosaic, a gentle reminder that no matter how ugly war's destruction, God had the power to make things beautiful again.

"What if some things can never be put back together? What if I have to go back to Harrisburg and tell Essie I couldn't find Wylie, or worse, what if he's dead?"

The familiar twinge of grief pierced her chest. Her goal of finding her father remained unspoken. No one but God knew of her intention to learn what had befallen him, and she knew the chance of finding him alive was almost zero. But if she could simply know for sure, perhaps the troubled dreams that invaded her sleep would come to an end.

"Lord, I can't bury him in my mind until I know." Her throat tightened, and burning moisture filled her eyes. "If I know he's with You, then I can be at peace."

Her heart turned over as she thought of her friend wondering all these years if her child was alive. Poor Essie tried to cling to the belief that Wylie would one day find his way to her. But with each month and year that passed, Charity saw the hope in Essie's eyes crumble a little.

"God, please help me find Wylie. I pray he's alive, but if he isn't, then help me know how to tell Essie."

If only Dale Covington had been able to give her a solid

lead to follow. Again, she recalled their meeting at the sawmill the other day. The man was not at all pleased to meet her. A twinge of shame nibbled at her heart. She'd marched in there all prepared to revile Mr. Covington with her scathing opinion of people who bought and sold other human beings. But a mysterious aura hung around the man like a cloak of grief that drew a haunted shroud over his eyes. She suspected he had his own version of war miseries. But what could be worse than expecting a loved one—a father, a brother, a husband, a sweetheart—to come home and having that wait stretch into months and years without any word? How did one finalize a bond with a person they loved and put their memories to rest?

She'd often thought it cruel and coldhearted to inform family members of their loved one's demise by telegram or letter. Words on paper seemed so heartless. But even a heartless letter would have been better than a state of oblivion.

Over the past several years, she'd seen and known many people who'd suffered a great loss through the war. Countless men came home blinded or missing a limb. Some could no longer work to support their families. Others were so devastated by what they'd witnessed, they turned to whiskey or opium to dull the pain. Others withdrew into themselves and no longer seemed to be the same person they once were.

Her conversation with Dale Covington became more puzzling every time she thought about it. How could he exude such melancholy over the loss of a house? When he spoke of it, his limp even became more pronounced. With the staggering number of casualties and destroyed lives as a result of the war, if all Mr. Covington lost was his house, he should count himself fortunate.

A twinge of regret poked her. Her parents taught her to

be compassionate and kindhearted, not cynical and judgmental. Her father always said to hear an entire matter before making up her mind. Otherwise, she was merely jumping to conclusions.

A lump filled her throat. "Papa was always right about such things." Her own whisper echoed in the emptiness of the room.

Mr. Covington did say he wished he could help find Wylie, and for some reason she couldn't explain, she believed him. As she'd left him that day at the sawmill, the expression in his eyes stayed with her. She was a journalist. She made her living with words. But she couldn't put her finger on the words to define what she saw in his eyes.

Her stomach growled, and she glanced at the dainty watch pinned to her bodice. Nearly six o'clock. She pushed away from the small desk and left her room. Perhaps she could give Mrs. Sparrow a hand.

The enticing aroma of roasting chicken greeted her halfway down the stairs. Three of the other boarders sat in the parlor awaiting supper, and Charity tried to remember their names. The county sheriff—she remembered his last name was Flint—reclined with one leg crossed over the other, a book in his hands. Another man—his name escaped her—read the *Juniper Springs Sentinel*. Did he work in the courthouse or land office? He might turn out to be a source of information if he had access to official records.

The third man she remembered. Tate Ridley slumped on the settee, impatience edging his features. Ridley was the most vocal of the boarders when Mrs. Sparrow introduced her as a magazine reporter. The man clearly didn't take to the idea of someone from the North reporting on the Reconstruction process. She almost suggested he write an article based on his own research and submit it, but she suspected the man couldn't read or write. When he looked over and saw her standing at the foot of the stairs, one corner of his mouth lifted, appearing more like a snarl than a smile.

Charity hurried to the kitchen door. "Mrs. Sparrow, what can I do to help?"

The plump woman straightened and brushed an errant lock of hair away from her face. "Well, you can start by calling me Hannah." She blotted perspiration from her forehead with the corner of her apron. "It's right nice of you to offer to help. Can you check the biscuits?"

"Certainly." Charity grabbed a towel and pulled the pan of golden brown biscuits from the oven. "Mmm, they're perfect. The dog usually tries to bury my biscuits."

Hannah chuckled. "It would be a sad thing if I couldn't make a decent biscuit after nearly forty years of practice." She deposited two fat roasted hens onto a large platter. "If you'll fill the water glasses, I'll put these birds on the table and call everyone to supper."

As soon as all the boarders were seated and Hannah asked God's blessing on the meal, conversation flowed as freely around the table as the serving vessels. Charity listened, trying to pick out the persons who might be the most willing to share information. The man whose name she couldn't remember gave her a syrupy smile and wiggled his eyebrows.

"Would ya pass the biscuits, please, Miss Galbraith."

Charity obliged him with a polite nod.

"Thank ya kindly, ma'am."

Tate Ridley snorted. "Looks like Arch got hisself some fancy manners. You tryin' to impress this here Yankee lady, Arch? Oh, that's right, I forgot. You're a Yankee yourself, ain't ya?"

The man Tate Ridley called Arch growled back. "There's nothing wrong with being polite. You could stand to learn some manners yourself, Ridley."

"Boys." Sheriff Flint held up his hand. The lamplight from the wall sconces glinted off his badge. "I'd be obliged if y'all didn't start anything I'd have to finish, 'cause I'd be mighty vexed if y'all interrupted my supper."

Hannah pointed her fork at both Ridley and Arch. "I've told you before. You two can disagree all you want, but not under my roof."

Ridley grunted and shoveled food in his mouth.

Arch shrugged. "Sorry, Miz Hannah."

Everyone ate in silence for a few minutes. Perhaps now was a good time to inquire if any of these local folks could aid her search.

"I wonder if any of you can answer a few questions for me." Several pairs of eyes looked her way. "You see, in addition to the articles I'm writing for the magazine, I'm also trying to locate someone. Perhaps some of you might know where I could find him."

Sheriff Flint took a sip of water. "What is this person's name?"

Charity blotted her lips with her napkin. "All I have is a first name—Wylie. He would be about twenty-four years old. He is a former slave, having been at Covington Plantation since 1859."

Tate Ridley glared at her and set his fork and knife down with a clatter. "You're lookin' for a darkie?"

"I'm looking for my friend's son whom she hasn't seen in eleven years."

Ridley demanded to know why she'd waste her time and called Wylie by a derogatory reference that Charity detested.

"Mr. Ridley, I would appreciate it if you would refrain from using that term." She mentally counted to ten and cut her glance to the others at the table. "Slave records were kept, but there was a fire and the records were destroyed.

Might there be any place else I could look? Were records of slave sales kept in any of the county offices?"

Frances Hyatt spoke up in her mousey little voice. "Miss Galbraith, why don't you ask Dale Covington? He might know."

"Yes, ma'am, I already did, but he couldn't recall the young man."

Another derisive snort came from Tate Ridley's side of the table. "*Young man!* Mighty highfalutin way to refer to a—"

"Tate. I believe the lady has already stated her request for you to mind your mouth and your manners."

All heads turned toward the kitchen door. Dale Covington stood in the doorway, his dark eyes narrowed and his jaw twitching.

Dale met Tate's glare without a blink. It wasn't the first time he'd locked horns with the crude fellow, but it normally occurred at the sawmill where they both worked. Most times Dale ignored the man's uncouth language, but not this time.

"Miss Galbraith is a lady, as are the rest of these women. Some of her questions may open wounds better left alone, but she's not being intentionally hurtful. You are. Keep your disrespectful opinions to yourself."

The ladies sat wide-eyed, and Miles Flint smirked, while Arch Wheeler and Elden Satterfield just kept eating. Tate Ridley pursed his lips and clenched his jaw. Charity Galbraith, however, turned a bright red and her eyes snapped with displeasure.

He turned to Hannah. "My apologies, Mrs. Sparrow, if I overstepped my bounds." He gestured over his shoulder. "I put your order from the mercantile on the kitchen worktable." He tugged the brim of his hat at the ladies and turned, striding through the kitchen to the back door.

"Wait."

He stopped and turned. Miss Galbraith hurried through the kitchen.

"I suppose I should thank you for coming to my defense, but what did you mean about my questions opening wounds?"

Before he could answer she rattled off her own indignant defense. "You may not approve of me being here, and perhaps my questions strike a nerve, but what I'm doing is in service to a friend."

"Well, isn't that noble of you." Dale folded his arms over his chest. "I may not be familiar with how things are done in Harrisburg, but around here right now, your questions might be considered inappropriate at best and dangerous at worst."

Her dark brown eyes shot sparks. "Dangerous! That's silly. The war is over."

He returned fire. "It's not over for everybody. Many Southerners are still fighting for their very existence, trying to regain some semblance of the way of life they once knew." He bit his tongue and refrained from spewing his own list of losses, lest it sound like self-pity.

Miss Galbraith stood with her hands on her hips. "Maybe they should have considered that before they seceded from the Union and started the war."

Dale's fingers curled into fists, and he stared hard at her. She had no idea how it was in Georgia during the fighting and its aftermath. He contemplated educating her in the ways of the South, but he had a notion the explanation would be a waste of breath, if she was like most hardheaded Yankees.

"There is some room for debate over which side was responsible for starting the war, but I'm talking about right now, today. You're here to write about the Reconstruction as well as find your friend's son. I'm only cautioning you to use discretion when you ask your questions."

She lifted her chin. "I'll ask whatever questions I need to in order to find Wylie. Your advice is interesting. I wonder if my friend would consider my inquiries offensive if they lead to locating her son."

Dale nudged his hat with his knuckle and blew out a stiff breath. "Miss Galbraith, I didn't say your cause is not a good one. It's a fine thing you're trying to do, even if it is a bit misguided and imprudent. I'm just suggesting you be careful who you ask. Not everyone will appreciate your devotion to your mission."

"Why is it imprudent? If your child was missing, wouldn't you welcome any and all help to find him?"

Her words slammed into him, nearly stealing his breath. Heat rose into his face, and his pulse pounded in his ears. A rush of blood fell into his belly.

She took a step forward, genuine concern tugging her brow. "Mr. Covington, are you all right?" Her tone lost its defiant edge and gentle warmth took its place.

All right? Was that a state of mind? He'd not considered for a very long time what it meant to be all right.

Miss Galbraith's dark eyes softened and a tiny crease formed between her brows. His chest squeezed. Had he noticed her enchanting eyes before? The slight blush in her cheeks? Her hair that glowed in the lamplight?

He stiffened his spine. When was the last time he looked at a woman in that way?

"Yes, I'm fine." He stepped backward toward the door. "Please, just be careful."

She cocked her head. Her piercing gaze seemed to penetrate his soul. "I will."

He stepped out the back door into the gathering dusk. The chilled autumn air pulled him back to consciousness. He shoved his hands into his pockets and hurried down the shadowy street. Miss Charity Galbraith was certainly the prettiest Yankee he'd seen in all the years since the onset of the war and afterward.

He slowed his pace. No point in hurrying home to an empty house. He welcomed the cool evening air on his face and took a deep breath. Someone had baked an apple pie. The crisp air laced with the homey scent spiked his loneliness. If only he could find a way to get past his anger. He didn't like the way it made him feel. Even Pastor Shuford suggested his bitterness poisoned him.

Miss Galbraith's image graced his thoughts again. He sincerely hoped she'd heed his advice, but caution threw a red flag in his face. Caring about a woman, especially a beautiful Yankee woman, spelled trouble. After all, old hostilities were hard to shake.

Chapter 5

"Have you gone soft in the head, Covington?"

Tate Ridley's caustic tone stirred Dale's ire, and ignoring him didn't appear to work. He turned to look the man in the eye. "I assume this is about your impolite behavior and crude language in the presence of ladies last evening."

"Ain't nothin' wrong with my way o' thinkin', but it 'pears like you done forgot which side you're on." Tate's sneer pulled his lips into a grotesque frown. "How come you was defendin' that Yankee woman? Are you forgettin' what her and her kind did to us?"

"Tate, you don't know what you're talking about." Dale brushed past him to continue inventorying the stack of logs. "Miss Galbraith didn't do anything to you. She is just doing her job, and I suggest you do yours."

"She's writin' for that magazine of hers. What do you think she's gonna write about?" Tate followed at Dale's heels, and a few other men stopped what they were doing to listen. "She's gonna make it sound like the South deserved what they got and how them Yankees is a bunch of heroes."

Dale heaved a sigh. "You've made me lose count again. Look, Tate. Save your foul language for the gutter rats with whom you associate. Miss Galbraith is a lady."

"She's a Yankee, and a Yankee is a Yankee." Ridley nearly spat the word. "They might've won the war, but that don't mean I hafta stand by and do nothin' while she belittles me and mine."

"What?" Dale gave him a sideways glance. "She didn't belittle you. Have you been drinking that moonshine again?"

Tate's face turned red. "She told me in her highfalutin' talk that she don't like the way I think."

"Simmer down, Tate. She's not the enemy." A twinge of guilt twisted in Dale's belly. Hadn't he thought of Miss Galbraith the same way? He turned his back to Tate and went through the motions of counting the logs, but his conscience nipped at him. "It's none of your business what she chooses to do for her friend, and I'm sure she'll write an honest account of the Reconstruction effort."

"Oh, you're sure o' that, are you? What's the matter with you? You turn into a blue belly?" Tate practically hissed over Dale's shoulder. "Don't you remember the fightin'? Don't you remember it was a Yankee minié ball that blew a hole through your leg? Did you forget how everybody sees you as a cripple now, and it's the Yankees' fault?"

Heat rushed through Dale, from his toes all the way to the roots of his hair. The stigma that dogged him every time he limped screamed in his face.

Cripple!

Bitter acid filled his gut. He clutched his pencil so tightly it snapped in half. Coming out of the war a lesser man spawned rage in his heart. The doctors told him his leg had healed as much as it would, and he should be thankful to have survived. They called him lucky.

Tate's questions were preposterous. No, he hadn't forgotten. He remembered every day, with every step he took, with every sympathetic look of pity.

"Ridley." Simon Pembroke's voice broke the grip Tate's words held on Dale. "Did you get that wagon loaded yet?"

"I'm gettin' to it right now."

"See that you do."

Tate leaned close to Dale's ear and growled under his breath, "She's a Yankee. Don't make no never mind that she's a woman. If you're a true son of the South, you'll see her for what she is."

Ridley sauntered off toward the partially loaded wagon, and Dale listened to his heavy-booted footsteps—his even-cadenced strides—fade away. Shards of animosity wedged themselves in his flesh, and the rancor he nurtured festered a little more.

"Dale."

He turned. Simon Pembroke stood a few feet behind him.

"Don't let Tate get to you. I could stand here and tell you he's a troublemaker, but coming from me it wouldn't mean much since I'm a Northerner." He sniffed. "But I'll tell you this. You're twice the man he is, and twice the worker." He pulled a fresh pencil from his pocket and handed it to Dale. "Thought you might need this."

Pembroke turned on his heel and strode back to the office. Dale's boss was a man of few words and didn't approve of wasting time with idle chat. Dale came to work, did his job, and accepted his pay at the end of the week. In the nearly six years since he'd worked at the sawmill, Simon had never said such a thing to him before.

Dale looked at the two pencils in his hand, one broken

and useless, the other whole and purposeful. And he did what anyone would do. He tossed the broken one away.

Dale spent the next hour counting and tallying the logs, but repeatedly had to admonish himself to concentrate. Tate's words rang louder than Simon's, and there was an element of truth in what Ridley said. Dale really didn't know for certain that Miss Galbraith's articles would reflect an honest disclosure of the Reconstruction process. Putting a splintered nation back together required the cooperation of all sides. Men bought lumber from Pembroke to reconstruct those buildings that were destroyed in the war. They carefully measured and cut, squared and nailed each board to create a solid structure. Likewise, each participant in the rebuilding of the nation must measure and ensure the trueness of what was built. If one didn't double-check for truth, imbalance would result. It stood to reason Miss Galbraith would write from a Northern perspective, but she had a responsibility to make sure her articles communicated the truth.

Last night he assumed any explanation to be a waste of breath. It might be wise to rethink that assessment. Perhaps he *should* enlighten her about the atrocities the South suffered. Politics aside, the cruelty of war destroyed much more than the Southern countryside. He just wasn't ready to share with her all the parts of his life that had been destroyed.

Charity stepped off the town doctor's porch and tucked her notebook into her pocket. Doctor Jonas Greenway had some interesting comments about the war and the reconnecting of all the states back into one nation, from a medical point of view. He'd seen and treated his share of war casualties from both sides. As he'd said so eloquently, "Soldiers don't bleed blue or gray. As a doctor, their blood was all the same to me." He told her he'd not prayed for the South or the North to win the war. He simply prayed for the war to be over. She'd filled several pages with notes.

Her only disappointment in the interview with the doctor was that he had no knowledge of a former slave named Wylie. Since he'd been away, attached to a regiment as a field surgeon, he'd not returned to Juniper Springs until after the Covington Plantation house burned.

She wished to interview Simon Pembroke as well, since the man hailed from Massachusetts. His take on the subject might prove interesting, but she didn't know how to approach the man without encountering Mr. Covington. She puzzled over the quandary.

After their confrontation in the boardinghouse kitchen ended with such a strange twist, for some reason, his feelings were important to her. After she'd recalled their heated discussion, she still couldn't put her finger on what had affected him to such a degree that he turned momentarily pale and speechless. But whatever the reason, it moved him visibly, and she desired to sit down with him again for another conversation.

Tate Ridley proved disconcerting. She found him rude and openly hostile, but he wasn't alone. Many Southerners still held deep resentment toward Reconstruction. She'd not anticipated encountering such hateful contention, but like it or not, she must include it in her articles.

Clearly, she didn't have a complete understanding of both sides. Until now, she'd only considered the perspective with which she and her mother had lived during the war and in the months to follow as they awaited word from her father. After her conversation with the doctor, chagrin pinched her as she acknowledged the thousands of Southern women who lost loved ones in the bloody conflict.

Pondering the depth of the research and inquires she

still needed, she couldn't put off contacting her editor any longer. Mr. Peabody tended to be a stickler for accuracy, so hopefully he'd agree to extend her deadline.

Charity stopped at the telegraph office and wrote out a brief message to the magazine editor indicating she'd need more time. The telegram cost much more than sending a letter, but she justified the expense, anticipating Mr. Peabody to be pleased with her meticulous fact-finding.

She stepped out the door of the telegraph office into the warm Georgia sunshine. Despite being late September, she didn't need a shawl at midday. The mountains just to the west of town shimmered with dappled autumn colors. Charity paused to appreciate the view. The mountains were strong, enduring for millennia, and even a tragedy like the war couldn't destroy them. They stood as a silent testament of God's power and strength. Charity took solace in the thought.

Up the street, the schoolchildren spilled out of the schoolhouse, scrambling for the best place in the yard to eat their lunch. She had an appointment to speak with the town lawyer, Ben Latimer, and she didn't want to be late. She checked the time. Thirty more minutes—time to stroll around the little town.

She backtracked and walked along a treed lane that led to the tumbling creek. Pembroke Sawmill stood on the opposite bank. On the far side of the lumberyard, Dale Covington wrangled a team of mules, hitching them to a massive log and driving them forward to drag the giant tree trunk into position for the saw blade. As she watched him, she imagined the drastic change the war brought to his life, and she admitted her shame to the Lord for her initial critical attitude in depreciating the man's losses. Enduring wounds on the battlefield and his house burning to the ground would be hard for anyone to bear.

Concealed by a holly bush, she watched him work. No doubt he'd once been a wealthy man if he owned a plantation. Now that he had no grand house or land, and no slaves to work for him, he earned his wage by the sweat of his brow. There was nothing careless or lazy in the way he did his job. For that, he earned her admiration.

She found it interesting that he stayed in Juniper Springs and found employment after the war, especially doing physical labor. How difficult had it been for him to remain in the area where he'd once been a prominent landowner? He must have known humiliation at having his social status jerked out from under him. Why did he stay here? Did he ever consider going someplace where nobody knew him? Her curiosity piqued, and she wondered if she'd dare ask him such questions, even in the name of research.

Charity scribbled as fast as she could push her pencil. Mr. Latimer, whose speech patterns identified him as a Southerner, gave her some insightful answers to her questions from the legal angle, explaining the process by which the legislature ratified the amendments required for readmission to the Union. In addition, he clarified the different periods of Reconstruction, outlining the nullifying of the state constitution before reorganization would take place.

Latimer leaned back in his desk chair. "Two years ago, the General Assembly expelled twenty-eight Negro members newly elected to the legislature because the state constitution didn't specifically give blacks the right to hold public office. Then they reversed their own decision on the fourteenth amendment, so the Federals returned and occupied the state again." He shook his head. "It's been a wickedly hard time for the people of Georgia."

Charity paused and tapped her pencil on her chin. "But why didn't they simply go along with the stipulations set down by the Federal court in the first place? It seems to me the Georgia Assembly made it harder on the people by continuing their rebellious posturing."

Latimer stroked his trimmed gray beard. "Some would agree with you, but you must remember Southerners are a proud people. They refused to admit defeat, and noncompliance with the demands of Congress was to them an act of pride and independence. Whether it was good for the people wasn't really taken into consideration."

Charity jotted down the lawyer's comments and closed her notebook. "I wonder if you could answer a couple of unrelated questions."

Latimer pulled out his pocket watch and flipped the cover open. "I have to be at the courthouse shortly, but I have a few minutes."

Charity breathed a quick prayer. "Would you happen to know of a former slave who worked at Covington Plantation before it burned? His name was Wylie."

Latimer frowned. "A slave, you say." His tone shifted. After being more than willing to supply information for her magazine articles, disapproval now peppered his voice. "A young lady like yourself shouldn't be pursuing a darkie. Why would your magazine send you on such an unseemly errand?"

Charity tightened her grip on her notebook, sliding her defensive bearing into place. "It has nothing to do with the magazine." She straightened her shoulders. "Wylie is my friend's son, and she longs to find him. I promised her I'd do everything I could."

The lawyer's brow furrowed into a V, and he shook his head. "It's unbefitting and crosses the line of propriety. I don't know any darkies by name. There's some that live on the other side of the river, but it's no place for a lady to go."

"I see." She stood and smoothed her skirt. The muscles

in her neck twitched, a warning sign that her temper was about to make an appearance. "Thank you for your time, Mr. Latimer."

He rose and came around the side of his desk and took her hand. His gracious demeanor returned. "If there's anything else I can do to help you, why you just come by and we'll have another chat."

After acting like her uncle Luther, showing gross disapproval of her mission to find Wylie, Mr. Latimer turned back into the benevolent sage. She walked toward the door before he could see her smirk. He strode past her to open the door in gallant fashion.

She paused, clutching her reticule in one hand and her notebook in the other. Turning to face the lawyer, she voiced one more hesitant question.

"By any chance would you know where the prisoner of war records are kept?"

Latimer rubbed his hand over his whiskered chin. "There was more than one prisoner of war encampment. The largest, of course, was at Andersonville. But I would suppose those are confidential military files. Why? Was this Wylie fellow a prisoner of war?"

A cold chill ran through her at the mention of Andersonville, the notorious prison where so many men died. The very thought of her father being imprisoned there nauseated her.

"I don't know about Wylie. I'm not even sure if he fought in the war. I'm looking for…a particular name."

"No." Latimer shook his head. "I'm not familiar with military courts. Perhaps if you contacted the war department in Washington."

She'd already done that five years ago, but they'd been unable to help since the records she sought were from the Confederacy.

"The man for whom I'm searching was a Union officer who was wounded and captured by the Confederate army in a battle here in Georgia."

The man arched his brow. "Oh?"

"His family is hoping for some kind of official statement...one way or the other."

"I'm truly sorry, Miss Galbraith." He sounded as if he suspected the person for whom she searched was dear to her. "I wouldn't know where such military records are kept, or if they are open to the public."

A lump grew in Charity's throat, and she forced a tiny smile. "Thank you, Mr. Latimer." An ominous burning in her eyes warned of eminent embarrassment. She hurried down the boardwalk.

How many dead ends must she encounter before she finally gave up?

Chapter 6

Charity sat at the kitchen table across from Hannah Sparrow. The heavenly aroma of sweet potato pies cooling on the windowsill seasoned the air in the room while they sipped their tea.

"So, now that you've been here almost two weeks, how do you like our little town?" Hannah pushed a plate heaped with oatmeal cookies in Charity's direction.

Charity relaxed in the cozy kitchen and in the comfortable presence of the woman. "It's lovely."

Hannah cocked her head. "That sounds as if there is something you'd like to add but don't want to offend anyone." She softened the remark with a smile that deepened the creases around her gray eyes.

"Well, I will admit I've encountered a few people who will probably not be added to my Christmas list." She took a nibble of a thick cookie and savored the cinnamony flavor.

Hannah's hearty laughter filled the kitchen. "At least you're honest." She selected a cookie and munched. "How is your research going?"

"Fairly well. I've spoken with a few people but have several more I'd like to interview, which reminds me"—she pulled her notebook from her pocket—"would you mind answering a few questions?"

"Me? Merciful heavens, child, couldn't you find anyone more interesting to talk to?"

Charity grinned. She would miss this sweet woman when it came time to go home. "I'm talking with people from all walks of life to get different perspectives."

Hannah reached for the teapot and refreshed her cup. "I can't imagine anything I have to say being of interest to anyone outside of Juniper Springs, but I'll help whatever way I can."

Charity opened the notebook and flipped several pages, but when she pulled out her pencil, she paused. "May I ask you about something else first, Hannah?"

"Of course. What is it?"

Charity explained about her mission to search for Essie's son and asked if Hannah knew of Wylie. The woman's eyes misted.

"No, I'm sorry, but I don't know him. I can't imagine how your friend felt being separated from her child. The practices associated with keeping slaves were pretty heartless." She reached across the table and patted Charity's hand. "I'll be praying you find this Wylie so his mama can hold him in her arms again." Her voice held a wistful note. "Dale Covington didn't remember him?"

"No, and after he explained why, I tried to understand. Things are just so different here from the way I grew up."

Hannah nodded. "Yes. Those differences are what tore our country apart."

Charity tapped her pencil on the blank page of her note-book. "Has the war and the Reconstruction affected your business here?"

"No." Hannah shook her head. "Not much. I had a couple of boarders who joined the state militia when the war first broke out. They were both killed. Owen Dinsmore died at Shiloh and Randall Kimber at Chancellorsville. Both of them had lived here at the boardinghouse for a few years.

"Two of the boarders I have now came after the war. Arch Wheeler is from New York and fought with the Union army. He came to take over at the land office after Randall was killed."

"Is that why Tate Ridley dislikes him so much?"

Hannah sighed. "I suppose. Those two haven't gotten along since the first day Arch arrived. Elden Hardy is from West Virginia. He doesn't talk much about the war, but a few suspect he was one who was denied citizenship in West Virginia because he aided the Confederacy."

Charity sipped her tea. "What about the town? You've been here most of your life, right?"

"I've lived in this area for thirty-five years. There were a lot of hardships during the war. With most of the able-bodied men from age sixteen to fifty off fighting, most of the work fell to the women and children. We didn't experience the food shortages to the degree that the cities did because most folks around here raised their own food, but there were things we couldn't get. Coffee was scarce and salt was rationed."

"How has the town changed since the war?"

"It's grown." Hannah reached for another cookie. "I remember when Juniper Springs wasn't much more than a half-dozen buildings. Now there are over thirty businesses. Simon Pembroke and a few others came to the area after the war and bought up land cheap."

Charity watched Hannah's eyes as she talked—"the windows to the soul" her mother used to say. Emotions lingered behind her landlady's eyes. "Are you saying these men came to make money on the rebuilding? Sounds like they're war profiteers."

Hannah splayed her hands on the table and shrugged. "I didn't mean to sound harsh, but I suppose they did come for the opportunities. Some resented it. Simon bought several hundred acres of timber and built the sawmill. But now he employs fourteen men—some work in the woods felling trees, and others work at the mill. Not only do these men have good jobs, Simon also provides a service we didn't have before the war. Four other new businesses opened in town, and over a dozen new families make this their home."

Charity laid her pencil down and leaned closer to Hannah. "Doesn't Tate Ridley work at the sawmill?"

"That's right."

Charity rolled the information over in her mind. "Tate doesn't like Arch because he's a Northerner who came here and took the job that one of the local men used to have, but Tate works for Simon, who is also a Northerner who came here, some say, to make money from the war." She cocked her head. "Isn't that a contradiction?"

Hannah rose and pumped more water into the kettle. "Tate says if a man is handing out money, he'll take it." She set the kettle on the stove and poked another piece of stove wood into the firebox. "To answer your question, yes, it seemed so to me as well, but Tate's ethics are his own business."

Charity picked up her pencil again. "So then I imagine Simon has made a lot of money supplying lumber for all the rebuilding over the past five years."

Hannah reclaimed her seat. "There wasn't a lot of destruction in this part of the state, but I think the sawmill has supplied building materials for some places south of here."

Charity tipped her head to one side. "Not a lot of destruction? But what about Covington Plantation?"

Dismay creased Hannah's face. "There were skirmishes, and certainly there were troops who passed through. But the worst were the scavengers toward the end of the war. They looted and burned several places, including Covington Plantation." She shook her head. "It was a terrible time. Even here in town we were in fear for our safety, but more from the scavengers than the actual fighting."

Charity jotted down some notes. She paused. How to address the next part of the conversation? She asked God for discretion and proceeded carefully. "Hannah, yesterday at church I noticed a large plaque on the wall with all the names of those men from this area who were killed in the war."

Hannah seemed to age a few years in the time it took to for Charity to speak her observation, as if the woman knew what Charity's next question would be.

"There are two names on the plaque—Matthew Sparrow and Edwin Sparrow. Were they your sons?"

A faraway look eased into Hannah's gray eyes. "Yes. I lost both my sons in the war. Matthew fell at Chickamauga in September of 1863. I traveled there to see his grave two years ago. It gave me a bit of peace to lay wildflowers there and ask God to take care of my boy."

Charity didn't interrupt. What could she say? How did one comfort a mother on the loss of her child? The ache she felt for Essie grew with Hannah's telling of her grief.

"I think Edwin died at Gettysburg." Her voice fell to a whisper. "So many fine young men, their lives snuffed out like a candle."

She *thought*? Charity couldn't force the words past her

lips. She sat without moving, barely taking a breath for fear of disturbing Hannah's deep, sad musing.

"I don't know where Edwin is buried." Hannah pressed her lips together and the tiny lines between her eyes deepened. "That plaque was put up just a few months ago." Her grief was underscored by her strained words. "People fussed and argued over it for five years."

How odd. Why would people not want to put up a memorial to their loved ones and friends who died in the war? Her puzzlement must have shown on her face, because Hannah explained.

"Some folks didn't want all the names engraved on the plaque, just those who fought for the Confederacy."

"Didn't everyone from Georgia fight for the Confederacy?"

"No." Extraordinary sadness taxed Hannah's voice. "It may come as a surprise to you, but there were plenty of Georgians who didn't believe in slavery, and therefore didn't support secession. Many of them fought for the Union. It caused some very hard feelings that some folks won't ever forget." Her eyes locked onto Charity's. "You see, my dear, the war didn't just divide the country. It divided communities, and"—the pitch of her voice rose unnaturally—"it even divided families."

Charity cringed inwardly, dreading to ask what she feared. "What do you mean?"

Tears filled Hannah's eyes. "While both my boys died in the war, Matthew fought for the Confederacy, but Edwin fought for the Union."

Charity couldn't breathe. How long had she considered her plight—not knowing what became of her father—the worst effect the war could have on a person? She was wrong.

* * *

Dale selected the straightest oak boards with the finest grain, meticulously sorting through the inventory. He stacked them carefully beside the maple already tucked onto the wagon bed. He glanced at the order again to confirm the correct number of board feet. Simon had called him aside this morning with instructions for Dale to work on this order alone. Dale didn't ask questions but merely set to work.

Despite trying to dismiss Simon's words last week, they lingered in Dale's memory. The opinion of a Yankee never mattered before. Why now? An element of gratification tickled his belly to know Simon had recognized how hard he worked.

He ran his hand over a length of red oak, the intricate grain creating a mosaic pattern beneath his fingers. He hefted the board and inspected it for trueness before adding it to the rest of the boards on the wagon. Checking the last of the oak off the work order, Dale initialed the paper and limped across the lumberyard toward the office.

Three men stood talking in the shadow of the mill. When Dale passed by, he caught snatches of their conversation.

"...let that Yankee woman know she ain't welcome."

Dale slowed his shuffling steps and listened. He identified the trio by their voices. Tate Ridley, Amos Burke, and Jude Farley exchanged comments in the cover of murky shadows between the mill and the pole barn.

"What about all them questions she's been askin' around, 'bout some darkie she's lookin' for?"

"And what do you suppose she's writin' in those articles of hers? All she wants to do is throw more mud on us Southerners."

"We don't need no Yankee, 'specially a woman, stirrin' up trouble. Bad enough the darkies are all uppity now."

"Someone needs to make an example out o' her."

"Meybe someone will."

Harsh laughter reached Dale's ears.

"Listen now. The brotherhood is meetin' this Saturday night. We'll talk about what needs doin'."

Dale had heard enough. With his hitched gait, he stepped over to the men. "Couldn't help overhearing you fellows. If you have any plans on harming, or even harassing Miss Galbraith, you'd do well to change them."

"What business is it of yours, Covington?"

Dale turned to face Tate Ridley. "It's my business when I hear what can be construed as making threats on a woman."

Ridley stepped up, inches from Dale's face. "I told you before, a Yankee is a Yankee. You're a traitor to your own people if you defend her."

Amos snorted. "Everyone in the county knows his brother-in-law was a bushwhacker durin' the war."

Dale's gut tightened. He and his sister, Auralie, had argued over Colton's involvement with the Union army. Regret pinched Dale. With their parents both gone, he had no other family. Their differences drove a deep wedge of alienation between them. He saw them when they came to town, and they never missed church, yet he'd barely spoken with Auralie and Colton for almost five years. Something he needed to address.

Tate sneered. "If you was a true gray-blooded Southerner, you'd be makin' plans to come to that brotherhood meetin' yourself, Covington." He pulled a pocketknife from his back pocket. "But I'll bet if I was to cut you, you'd bleed blue, wouldn't you?"

Dale pointed his clipboard at Tate and then swung it to

include Amos and Jude. "Leave Miss Galbraith alone or I'll have something to say about it."

"Ooh, ain't ya skeered, boys?" Amos guffawed. "This here crippled man's gonna have somethin' to say."

Dale jerked his thumb over his shoulder toward the mill. "There's three more orders in there that need to be filled today. If you boys are finished taking your break, I'd appreciate some help." He turned and gimped toward the stairs that led to the office. Anger impeded his steps as laughter followed him.

Simon Pembroke sat at his desk and looked up when Dale entered. "You're finished with that order already?"

Dale handed his boss the clipboard. "I picked through every piece of oak and maple to find the straightest boards, and there's not a knot in one of them."

Simon bobbed his head. "That's fine. This order is going to Lucas Adair, and you know how persnickety he is."

Had Dale not been so incensed by the three men in the lumberyard, he might have smiled at Simon's accurate portrayal of the cabinetmaker. "It's loaded and ready to go."

Simon pulled himself around in his chair. "Sit down, Dale." He gestured to the place next to the desk. "I want to show you something."

Dale sat and watched as Simon unrolled a map and anchored the corners down. He pointed to a section Dale knew well. "I understand you once helped survey this acreage."

Dale examined the map. "Yes, I did. It was before the war, though. Ten years ago. My father attempted to purchase this"—he ran his finger across the map between two points already marked—"this is the boundary line to my brother-in-law's land, and this tract is prime timber."

"I know. I bought it last week." He rolled up the map and stuck it in a drawer. "It's going to mean I'll be away from here two or three days a week for a while, and I'm going to need a foreman to oversee the mill operation." He leaned back in his chair. "You're my first and only choice."

The unexpected offer raised Dale's eyebrows. "You want me to be your foreman?"

"It shouldn't surprise you. I've watched the way you work, the diligence you put into everything you do. You certainly aren't lazy." Simon reached into one of the desk's cubbyholes and extracted a key. He laid it in front of Dale. "And I believe I can trust you."

"But you're—I'm—"

Simon smiled, something Dale had never seen him do.

"I'm blue and you're gray?" Simon shook his head. "Not anymore." He extended his hand.

Dale hesitated. He'd managed to put aside his animosity working for this man with the New England accent and do his job. Simon had always dealt fairly with him. He picked up the key and shook Simon's hand.

Strange. At one time he would have looked down his nose at someone like Simon Pembroke. Not long ago he'd have considered the man's offer an insult. As he descended the stairs and hitch-stepped across the yard, he took a moment for introspection.

Hard work, perseverance, and dependability had reaped him a reward, and it felt good.

Chapter 7

The general store, while small in size, supplied everything on Charity's list. The balding storekeeper and his wife—did he call her Sweet Pea?—served her with gracious smiles, unlike some of the receptions she'd received from a few other folks.

Since she'd decided to extend her stay and the evenings were growing cooler, she purchased a heavier shawl, a sturdier bonnet, and a pair of warmer stockings. As she browsed the store, she added a package of hairpins, a bar of castile soap, a new nib for her pen, and a box of envelopes to the collection of goods in her arms.

As she walked toward the counter, trays of stationery caught her eye. The supply she'd brought with her was dwindling. Just as she picked up a box of paper, the door to her left opened and a man entered carrying two crates, one stacked atop the other. The door swung against her arms, sending sheets of stationery fluttering like autumn leaves in their descent to earth. In her effort to snatch her other purchases before they scattered across the floor, Charity bent and reached out at the same instant the man with the crates did. The top crate crashed to the floor, spilling its contents of ribbons and sewing supplies. In the space of a heartbeat, Charity recognized Dale Covington at the very moment their heads collided with a *thunk*.

Bumped off balance, she plunked down on her backside, holding one hand to her head.

Mr. Covington grabbed for the elusive papers as they sailed in the breeze from the open door. His boot landed on Charity's bar of soap and slid out from under him, sprawling his legs in opposite directions. Unable to regain his balance, he joined Charity in an ungainly position on the floor.

The storekeeper came rushing over. "Well, land o' Goshen, boy, what in tarnation's goin' on here?"

Heat rushed into Charity's face, and her head smarted. She risked a glance at Mr. Covington seated a few feet from her. A stricken expression of mortification surfaced across his face. A giggle bubbled up from her stomach. She tried to hold it back, fearing her display of humor might offend him. But the mirth refused containment and came puffing out her pursed lips. Once escaped, the laughter mocked her effort to suppress it by building into uncontrolled gales.

"I'm sorry—" It was no use. The words came out in a sputter, and she surrendered to a torrent of giggles.

Finally, a deep-throated chortle joined her in a hilarious duet. She caught her breath, wiped her eyes, and looked over at Mr. Covington. The moment their gazes connected, the laughter started anew. After watching his dark, brooding expression since she'd arrived in town, she didn't think the man knew how to laugh, but she was wrong. The sound rippled through her like a symphony.

The storekeeper stood with his hands on his hips. "Well,

I declare, if you two ain't a sight. I don't reckon either of you is hurt, judging by the cacklin' goin' on." He shook his head. "Well, don't just set there, boy, help the lady to her feet."

Weak from the expression of unbridled humor, Mr. Covington held onto the doorframe to steady himself. He reached down and cupped her elbow, supported her forearm, and lifted her. Remnants of a smile lingered on his face.

"Are you quite all right, Miss Galbraith?"

"I'm fine, Mr. Covington, but under the circumstances"—she gestured to the scattered merchandise—"I don't think it would be improper for you to call me Charity."

"I do apologize...Charity."

"Please don't. I haven't laughed so hard in years."

A tiny, lopsided grin tipped one side of his mouth. "Me either." He stooped and began picking up the sheets of paper, stacking them in a neat bundle.

"Mr. Covington, I—"

"Dale." A momentary glitter in his eye made her catch her breath.

Butterflies danced in her stomach. "Dale." She took the collected stationery he handed her. "I fear the last time we talked I may have come across as a bit abrasive. Please know that wasn't my intention."

He scooped up her package of hairpins and bar of soap. "No offense taken."

She blew out a short sigh of relief and snatched up the pair of stockings while he gathered the ribbons and sewing supplies that had fallen from the crate. As he did so, she noticed he barely limped at all.

"Dale, would you have time to talk?"

He straightened and shook his head. "As soon as I get these things put out, I have deliveries to make."

"I see." She watched as he retrieved the remaining articles from the floor. "I've come to realize I've been looking at the war from only one side. Being here has opened my eyes, and there is much more research needed before I can write unbiased articles."

He handed her the box of envelopes. "Glad to hear it."

Hope sprang up in her chest. "Does that mean you're willing to talk with me at another time?"

He hesitated and withdrew a bit into the Dale Covington she encountered on her first day there. Regret tugged at her. The glimpse of Dale she caught when he laughed was much more desirable.

She hugged her purchases to her. "Sunday afternoon?"

He shrugged. "I suppose." He stacked the two crates again and lifted them. "Sunday afternoon, then."

An odd thread of anticipation tiptoed through her. Three more days.

The sound of the congregation singing lifted Charity's heart as she took her place beside Hannah Sunday morning. "All hail the power of Jesus' name, let angels prostrate fall. Bring forth the royal diadem, and crown Him Lord of all." The praise made her spirit soar.

She settled in with her Bible on her lap and flipped the pages to the text Pastor Shuford announced, Luke chapter fifteen. As he began to speak about the parable of the lost son, Charity's heart pinched. She pictured Essie, standing and watching for her son the way the father in the parable did.

Lord, please be with me as I search, and lead me to Wylie.

Her silent prayer brought Dale to her mind. Even if he

couldn't remember Wylie, perhaps he could suggest somewhere to look. The expression that had come over him and darkened his eyes the first time she'd inquired still haunted her. What if there was something more ominous behind that look? Dare she bring up the subject again?

She hadn't seen him before the service started. She turned her head as far as she dared without people sending her disapproving frowns. From the corner of her eye, she caught sight of him sitting near the back. She pulled her focus back to the preacher, but Dale's presence a few rows behind her proved quite distracting.

After the closing hymn and prayer, Charity looked up and found Dale standing beside her.

"Good morning, Mrs. Sparrow. Charity."

A warm flush filled Charity's cheeks. Did he notice? She turned to her landlady who had a mischievous twinkle in her eye. "Hannah, would it be all right with you if Dale came to the boardinghouse later this afternoon? I have a few more questions I'd like to ask him."

The corners of Hannah's lips twitched, and she reached for Dale's arm. "Why don't you come for Sunday dinner, Dale? We'd love to have you."

Charity hiccuped. What did Hannah think she was doing? Playing matchmaker?

Dale raised his hand in protest. "Oh no, I don't want to put you out."

"You'd do nothing of the kind. I have a pot roast simmering, and there is plenty to go around." She patted his arm. "You come right on. I made an applesauce cake for dessert."

A rush of warmth pervaded Charity's middle. Her other meetings with Dale had been more businesslike. Well, except the unplanned meeting they had in the general store. But sitting next to him at dinner? Wouldn't that be considered too...friendly? Of course, dinner at the boardinghouse with eight other people around the table wouldn't exactly be an intimate tête-à-tête. She smiled.

"You can't say no to Hannah's pot roast and applesauce cake."

A boyish grin tipped his mouth. "It's been a long time since I had a Sunday dinner like that. I'd be happy to accept."

Why was her stomach doing flips? Charity reprimanded herself, but her heart still rat-tat-tatted like a dizzy woodpecker.

"That was the best meal I've had in years, Hannah." Dale still stumbled over calling the woman by her first name, but she'd insisted. He held up his hand at her offer of another piece of applesauce cake. "I couldn't eat another morsel." He grinned. "But I wish I could."

When Charity began picking up plates and serving bowls, Hannah flapped her hands. "I'll do that. You young folks go on. Why don't you sit out on the back porch? It's nice and sunny out there, and you won't be disturbed." She spoke the last part of her statement rather pointedly.

Dale slid a sideways glance at Margaret Ferguson. The woman had blatantly aimed all her attention at him during dinner, much to Dale's chagrin. A childish pout poked her bottom lip out, and she marched from the dining room with a huff.

"Well then, I suppose we should go out to the porch." The pitch of Charity's voice rose a notch, along with his own level of apprehension. Such nonsense. He'd spoken with her before. They'd even banged heads and laughed about it together while sitting on the floor. Why was this different?

She picked up her notebook and preceded him through the kitchen. He held the back door for her while they stepped out to the porch. He glanced from one end of the porch to the other. No chairs. The only place to sit was a swing just wide enough for two. He could have sworn Mrs. Sparrow kept a couple of wicker chairs out here. Didn't he remember seeing them when he came to deliver her groceries? He tossed a look over his shoulder at the back door that stood ajar. Inside, Hannah hummed as she bustled about the kitchen. The woman was a sweet, loving person, but she was sly!

Dale held the chain of the swing until Charity sat. Uneasiness flooded the space between them, so thick it felt like a tangible thing. She opened her notebook and turned to a blank page.

"Do you mind talking about the war? I'd like to hear your story."

A lightning bolt ripped through him. The only person he'd really talked with about his experiences in the war was Pastor Shuford, and the preacher's words came rushing back to him.

"I fear the bullet that injured your leg did less damage than the resentment and animosity you nurture. Don't you see, son? Your old wound has been trying to heal for six years, but your bitterness is making you a cripple."

He stiffened and looked away. If he'd known this conversation would turn personal, he'd have turned down the invitation. He expected general questions about politics and Georgia's readmission to the Union. He curled his fingers into fists. Talking about his private pain he'd worked so hard to bury wasn't something he was ready to do. Was that true? Had he tried to bury it, or had he done what Pastor Shuford had said? Nurturing the bitterness took more ongoing effort than burying it.

Charity's quick intake of breath defined her regret. "I'm sorry." Her voice was quiet and gentle. "It wasn't my in-

tention to make you uncomfortable. It's just that I've realized in the time I've been here that everyone has their
own story—their own individual experience that isn't the
same as anyone else's. My own experience is much different from yours, I'm sure."

He'd not thought of her having an experience from the
war. Except for Gettysburg, he assumed Pennsylvania had
remained relatively untouched by the war.

"When my editor gave me this assignment, I hoped to
use part of my time here in Georgia to look for information—" Her voice tightened. "About my father."

He turned to look at her more fully and saw deep pain
in her eyes. "Your father? I thought you were looking for
a young slave."

"I am." Her eyes glistened. "But I also want to find out
what happened to my father. He was a Union officer. The
few letters he sent said he'd been engaged in several battles in Virginia, Tennessee, and Georgia. My mother and I
received word that he'd been wounded and taken prisoner,
but that was the last we heard." A single tear slid down
her face, and her voice dropped to a hushed whisper. "He
never came home."

A tiny ache kindled within him as he listened to her bare
her heart—the pain of not knowing, or even having a grave
to visit. The tremor in her voice gripped him. Her determination to seek out the prisoner of war records and learn,
once and for all, what happened to her father, gave him a
glimpse of the passion with which she persevered. Her can-
didness pried away his hold from the horror of his memories. Pastor Shuford said it was time he talked about it.

He took a fortifying breath. "When I came home, the
house was nothing but a burned-out shell. Nearly all the
slaves were gone, the land in ruins with no way to plant
or harvest a crop. Scavengers had looted the place. They

took…everything. The graves—" He clamped his jaw so tightly it hurt, and he recognized something for the first time. That sensation of hardness that crawled up his gut and into his throat wasn't sorrow. It was anger. Bitter, acid rancor. He forced his hands to relax and concentrated on breathing evenly. After a minute, he continued.

"Both of my parents died during the war. My mother from apoplexy, and my father from consumption. The gravestones had been knocked over and trampled." But the loss of his home wasn't what carved the deepest scars into his heart. "My—"

A vise strangled him. No, he wasn't ready yet to speak of the vilest atrocity. There were some things a man couldn't express.

Besides, why should it matter to him that a Union officer didn't come home? Between the fighting itself and those who died in the prison camps or from disease, over 680,000 men didn't come home. He tried to harden his heart, but he couldn't get around the truth. He did care. He cared about her pain, he cared about her search, and— God help him—he cared about her. How could he do that?

It wasn't reasonable to blame Charity. She didn't burn his home or rip the most precious thing in his life from him. Likewise, he wasn't responsible for whatever happened to her father.

Her soft voice broke through his thoughts. "Dale, you don't have to say any more."

He turned to look at her, and unshed tears clung to her lashes. His gaze dropped to the notebook in her lap. She hadn't written a single word.

They sat in gentle silence, swaying to and fro on the swing. Shadows lengthened and the air chilled.

"I wondered if you'd thought of anywhere I might look for Wylie."

Reference to the former child-slave didn't sicken him the way it had with her first inquiry. He released a sigh. "No." He shifted on the swing to look at her. "I know I've mentioned this before, but I want to caution you again. Some people won't take kindly to you asking around about a slave, especially since you're—"

"A Yankee?" Her voice held a hint of animation.

"Yes." He stood. "It's getting late. I should go."

She rose, and they walked to the top of the porch steps where he paused before descending. "Charity, may I take you to dinner one night next week?"

Her smile sent the shadows into hiding. "I'd like that."

Chapter 8

Charity poked her head inside the door of the land office. "Mr. Wheeler?"

The man rushed around the side of the desk. "Yes, yes, please come in. And call me Arch." His silly grin stretched across his face. "After all, we sit at the same supper table every night, don't we?" He pulled a chair out from the corner. "Please have a seat."

Arch's demonstrative manner took her by surprise. At the boardinghouse he spent most of his time sparring with Tate Ridley. The two of them reminded her of a pair of alley cats, hissing and spitting, yowling their opinions.

He grabbed his desk chair and maneuvered it to face Charity's. He plunked down in the chair and leaned forward. "It's nice that we finally have some time alone to get better acquainted."

Time alone? Charity wasn't sure what Arch had in mind, but the purpose for her visit was purely business.

She scooted her chair backward a couple of inches and quickly pulled out her notebook.

"Would you have time to answer a few questions, Mr. Wheeler?"

A crestfallen expression drooped the man's mustache. "Arch."

She allowed a placating smile. "Arch." She pointed to several file cabinets lining the wall. "Are all these land records?"

"Most. Some are financial documents, property taxes, things like that."

"I see. I understand a lot of people lost their land after the war."

Arch nodded. "Mm-hmm. When the slaves were turned loose, a lot of the big landowners didn't have anybody to work their land and didn't have the money to pay for help. No slaves, no crop. No crop, no money. No money, they can't pay their taxes. People came in droves after the war looking for bargains. They paid the taxes; they bought the land. Simple as that."

Simple maybe, for the buyers. "But what about the people who lost their land, their homes. What did they do? What happened to them?"

The words no sooner passed her lips than she realized she was talking about Dale. She squirmed with discomfiture, but apparently Arch didn't notice.

"A lot of the landowners or their heirs died in the war. Many of the ones who survived were destitute." He rose and pulled open one of the file drawers, thumbing through some of the folders. "A few went upriver or out west. Some took up with relatives in the city. Some just left and were never heard from again."

"But not all. Dale Covington didn't leave. Why did he stay? Something must have kept him here."

"I guess you'd have to ask him about that."

"And the land that was sold for taxes, what is it being used for now?"

Arch pulled out a few files and leafed through the paperwork. He ran his finger down several pages and then stepped over to a large map pinned to the wall. He traced a block of land. "This area right here has been planted in fruit trees and pecan trees." He slid his hand westward on the map. "Here's a pretty large tract turned into grazing land for cattle." He consulted the documents in his hand again and pointed to the corresponding area. "Simon Pembroke bought up several hundred acres of timber that goes from here all the way up to here." He gave the remaining papers in his hand a cursory glance before gesturing back toward the map. "Some of this land has been parceled out into tenant farms. A brick foundry was built on a stretch of land east of here on the other side of the river."

She closed her notebook. "So, Mr. Wheeler—Arch, do you know what happened to the slaves who worked on these plantations?"

Arch shrugged and closed the file drawer. "Most just run off, I suppose. A few stayed and indentured themselves. You still looking for that friend of yours?"

"He is my friend's son. I've never met him."

A flicker of disdain crossed Arch's face. "You gonna write about that in your high-toned magazine?" His question irritated her, but she had to admit his insinuation was true. Since the majority of *Keystone's* readers came from the upper echelon of society, they likely wouldn't care about one former slave and his mother. Charity chose to ignore Arch's question.

She rose and tucked her notebook under her arm. "Thank you for your time, Arch. I appreciate the information."

"Come by any time." He followed her to the door. "It's

easier to talk here where we aren't disturbed than at the boardinghouse. We can…get to know each other better." He waggled his eyebrows.

Charity bit her lip to refrain from telling him she had nothing to discuss with him that required privacy. Instead, she forced a tight smile. "Good day, Arch."

She swept out the door with her eyes cast heavenward, hoping she hadn't encouraged him in any way.

The courthouse—rather stately for a small town like Juniper Springs—occupied the space between two majestic oak trees next door to the sheriff's office. Autumn foliage glistened bronze, pumpkin, and scarlet in the sunshine, but a brisk wind pressed Charity to gather her shawl tighter. A gust loosened several dozen leaves and showered them down across the front steps of the courthouse. Charity pulled the heavy door open and slipped inside out of the wind.

The modest lobby opened to expose four doors and a staircase. Charity glanced around and found the last door on the right boasted the title Records on the glass. She opened the door tentatively and peeked inside. A clerk stood at a counter helping a man and a woman with some documents.

"I'll be right with you, miss."

Charity smiled and nodded. "No hurry."

The woman, who wore a plain bonnet and gray dress with purple trim, turned to stare over her shoulder at Charity. She leaned close to the man and whispered something Charity couldn't hear.

Suddenly self-conscious, Charity reached up to make sure the wind hadn't dislodged her hairpins or deposited a stray leaf in the brim of her bonnet. Finding nothing amiss, she stood to one side until the couple moved to an adjacent table. The clerk turned to her.

"What can I do for you?"

"Good afternoon. I'm Charity Galbraith, and—"

"See, George." The woman at the table nudged her husband. "I told you it was her—that Yankee woman whose been goin' around town askin' a lot o' questions."

The man looked up from the papers he was reading and squinted at her. Charity squirmed under their scrutinizing stares but continued on with the clerk.

"I hope you can help me. I'm conducting a search for a young man, a former slave. His name is Wylie, and he worked at Covington Plantation. I understand the house burned and their records were destroyed. Were there any records kept on file here?"

The clerk's eyes darkened with suspicion. "Slave records?"

"Yes." Charity lowered her shawl to her elbows and drew her notebook from under her arm. "I'm specifically looking for records of slave auctions or the private buying and selling of slaves. Birth and death records, perhaps?" She slid her gaze sideways and found the couple at the table still staring.

"The plantation owners usually kept all those records."

"Yes, I know." Impatience nipped at her. "But as I said, the house at Covington Plantation burned. Was the buying and selling of slaves recorded here?"

"If a colored was sold, the new owner would have a record of it."

Charity's fingers tightened around her notebook in frustration. "But I don't know if Wylie was sold. That's why I'm here. Do such records exist?"

The clerk lifted his shoulders. "What difference does it make? Lincoln freed all the coloreds, so even if this boy was sold, he's free now."

Charity gritted her teeth and mentally counted to ten.

"If Wylie was sold, perhaps whoever bought him can tell me where he went after the war."

She glanced toward the table where the couple continued to regard her with distrust.

"I don't know where records like that might be, 'cept with the buyers." Contempt dripped from the clerk's voice, and his steely eyes didn't blink.

Dale's warning rang in her ears. She pursed her lips and looked down at her unopened notebook. The reception she'd received couldn't get much colder. She might as well dive all the way in.

"I wonder if I might ask another question."

The man responded with a nearly imperceptible lift to his whiskered chin.

"I'm also searching for battlefield maps and records of battles fought in Georgia, specifically with regard to casualties and prisoners."

The clerk made a rude sound, sucking on his teeth. "Military records are sealed. Someone like you wouldn't be given access."

She clamped the notebook tightly, praying she wouldn't throw it at the man. "Well, thank you for your time." She sent a forced smile to the couple at the table. "Have a nice afternoon."

She turned and marched to the door. As she turned the brass knob, the woman at the table spoke. "She sure got a lot o' nerve, don't she?"

If only the woman knew how much nerve Charity required at this moment to keep from speaking what was on her mind.

Dale knocked on the front door of the boardinghouse and brushed imaginary lint from his cuff. Charity opened the door, rendering Dale momentarily speechless. He'd seen her numerous times over the past three weeks, but there was something different about her tonight. Perhaps it was her smile.

"Good evening, Charity."

"Good evening." She held the door open. "Please come in. I just have to get my wrap."

He stepped inside. Would it be too forward to tell her how lovely she looked?

She returned a moment later carrying an ivory shawl. He took it from her and unfolded it, placing it over her shoulders. A hint of lavender teased his senses.

Her eyes widened and her lips parted as she looked up at him. A silent reprimand slinked through him. If the gesture surprised her, he'd not been acting enough like a gentleman. Something he intended to change.

They stepped out onto the porch and Dale offered her his arm. "Shall we go?"

A tiny smile tipped her mouth, and she placed her hand in the crook of his elbow.

They crossed the street and started down the boardwalk. The hotel restaurant sat between the general store and the hotel itself. Dale opened the door and ushered Charity inside. They paused for a moment while Dale scanned the room, seeking a table where they could speak with a certain amount of privacy. He noticed George and Henrietta Ludwig sitting at a small table halfway across the room. Both had stopped eating and sat glaring in Dale and Charity's direction. He felt Charity stiffen.

When he glanced down, her chin rose slightly and a muscle along her jaw twitched. Tracing her line of vision, it appeared the Ludwigs and Charity had made a less than cordial acquaintance with each other.

He leaned his head down and spoke close to her ear.

"It seems a little crowded in here. Would you rather go to Maybelle's Café?"

Relief washed over her expression. "Yes, I'd like that."

Back out on the boardwalk, they strolled past several buildings before either of them spoke.

"Is it safe to assume you've met George and Henrietta?"

Charity shrugged. "We weren't formally introduced, but I, um…ran into them at the courthouse a couple of days ago."

She didn't need to say any more. The Ludwigs were among those who declared the war would never be over for them, even though they'd lost far less than most. An urge to put the couple in their place needled Dale.

Lord, please keep reminding me that I'm not responsible for anyone's opinions or attitudes but my own.

He placed his hand protectively atop Charity's as they continued toward Maybelle's. Enticing aromas greeted them at the door of the café.

"Smells like the special this evening is chicken." Dale's mouth watered as he steered Charity toward a table in the corner. Maybelle brought them coffee and took their order.

Dale cleared his throat. "Have you been able to find any information about your father?"

A tiny crease between her brows deepened, lines of sorrow marring her countenance. She shook her head, and Dale instantly regretted asking.

He changed topics. "I've been thinking about this slave you're searching for." He took a sip of coffee. "My father and I had more than one argument about the slaves, but as long as he was alive, I had little to say about their treatment."

Charity's warm brown eyes studied him, as if she tried to read his thoughts.

He intertwined his fingers. "I was of the opinion the

slaves would be more productive if they had better food and housing, but Father disagreed. Loudly. He did everything loudly."

Charity's expression softened into an understanding smile. He had to be truthful. "When you showed up here and started asking your questions, I began to realize my position on the slaves was to get more work out of them if we fed them better." He lowered his eyes and toyed with his fork. "Many of my beliefs and attitudes were based on how I was raised."

Maybelle brought plates of baked chicken and golden biscuits, along with a small dish of butter and a crock of honey.

"Anything else I can get for you folks?" She refilled their coffee cups.

"I don't think so." Dale sniffed. "This smells wonderful."

Maybelle nodded with a pleased grin and bustled away. Dale bowed his head and asked God's blessing on their meal.

They began to eat, and Charity looked across the table at him with a penetrating gaze of comprehension. "What changed your mind?"

He stopped chewing for a moment. How could she tell? He swallowed hard and pushed his chicken around on the plate with his fork.

"The war had already started. I'd been away for months. I'd barely received word that Father was ill when the telegram came saying he'd died. I couldn't get home for the funeral, but I was told they laid him to rest beside my mother." He knew he wasn't answering her question, but she didn't interrupt, as if encouraging him to take his time.

He buttered a biscuit, but then laid it on his plate without taking a bite. He ran his finger around the rim of his coffee cup. "I had been with Major General Cleburne for some time, but when President Davis relieved General Johnston and appointed General Hood to take his place, Hood needed reinforcements. I was sent, along with part of our regiment to attach to Hood's in July of 1864. The Yankees were threatening to overrun Atlanta, and our job was to stop them at Peachtree Creek."

He sat back, the memory flooding over him, as it often did.

"The fighting at Peachtree Creek was fierce, and we were all exhausted. I was hit in the side." He rubbed the place with his fingers. "I tried to crawl to some bushes, but I was hit again, this time in the leg. I couldn't move, and I knew I was going to die."

Charity covered her mouth with her fingers.

"There was a soldier—I'd not known him before I joined Hood. He was a black man, no doubt a slave who'd been sent to fight in the place of his master. He bent over me and told me I was going to be all right. He picked me up in his arms like I was a child and carried me to some thick underbrush until the battle was over. I drifted in and out of consciousness, but every time I opened my eyes, he was there. He made some kind of poultice for my wounds. I remember him talking the whole time, but he wasn't talking to me. He was talking to Jesus, asking Him for strength to carry me and asking Him to let me live. That man carried me for two days until we reached a regiment that had a doctor." He looked across the table at Charity. Tears shimmered in her eyes.

"I never knew his name."

Chapter 9

Charity took Dale's arm and a flutter of butterflies turned loose in her stomach. She clutched her shawl with her free hand. Darkness had fallen and the lantern light that spilled over the boardwalk cast ghostly shadows against the buildings as Charity and Dale strolled past. The evening air held a chill, but walking next to Dale felt warm.

The short route from the café to the boardinghouse didn't allow much time for conversation, but Dale had spoken volumes over dinner, even when he sat silently poking at his food with his fork. In those moments when their gazes locked, his eyes cracked open the door to his innermost secrets, and Charity caught a brief peek at the man he was on the inside. A surprisingly compassionate person hid behind the sullen, brooding expression she'd met the first day she made his acquaintance. As they made their way through the gathering night, the man he was on the outside barely limped at all.

"I've enjoyed the evening, Dale. Thank you." She looked up at him. The lanterns were spaced far enough apart that the light danced across his face and then hid as they moved along.

His brow dipped in consternation. "Charity, I've never told anybody what I told you tonight, about how that black soldier saved my life."

A warm flush twined up her neck and into her face. "Then I feel very honored that you would confide such a remarkable experience to me."

"But are you going to…write about it?"

"Not if you don't want me to."

He gave a short nod, seemingly satisfied that he could trust her not to betray his confidence.

"It's not that I don't want to give credit to that soldier. I should." His voice dropped off, almost as if he was speaking more to himself than to her.

Was he embarrassed to admit a black man had saved him?

He halted and turned to face her. "Charity, there is more to that story that I didn't tell you. During those two days that soldier took care of me and carried me to safety, I never once spoke to him." Self-deprecation laced his tone. "He'd offer me a drink, and I grunted and nodded. He knew I was in a lot of pain, so we stopped to rest often, but he rarely spoke directly to me, other than telling me I was going to be all right. He kept up a running conversation with the Lord, though. I listened to him pray for two days, and he talked to Jesus like a best friend."

He dropped his gaze to the boardwalk. "Charity, I never asked his name. I never even thanked him." He turned his head as if looking her in the eye as he admitted his shortcomings was too difficult.

Charity waited. An owl hooted in the distance and a breeze stirred the air.

"I wish I knew his name, and I wish I'd shaken his hand." A sigh that sounded more like a groan escaped his lips, and he shook his head.

She reached out and touched his cuff. "Dale, have you ever read the parable of the two sons?"

He shook his head. "I don't think so."

"Jesus told a story about a man who had two sons. He went to the first son and told him to go work in the father's vineyard, and the son refused. Later, the son repented and went and worked in the vineyard."

She paused to give him time to digest the scenario. "Then the father went to the second son and told him to go work in the vineyard, and the son said he would do it, but he didn't."

A frown dipped Dale's mouth. "What does that have to do with the soldier who took care of me?"

A fleeting prayer winged toward heaven. *Please, don't let me offend him, Lord.*

"Which one of the sons did the father's will?"

Dale shrugged. "The first one, but I still don't understand."

"You might have started out with a hard heart, but your heart has changed."

A scowl interrupted his features.

She prayed he wasn't angry. "God knows we're going to stumble and fall once in a while, but He doesn't leave us where we fall. He picks us up and gives us another chance."

His expression mellowed and softened, and finally he gave a slow nod. "I understand what you're saying. I'll have to do some thinking about it."

The lanterns hanging from the front porch of the boardinghouse came into view, and Dale's steps slowed. "Would you allow me to read your articles when you've finished writing them?"

She arched her eyebrows. "You want to proofread them, or don't you trust me to write impartially?"

He chuckled. "I'm curious. In your short time here you've been quite thorough in your research. From what I can see you've interviewed quite a few people."

She peeked at him from the corner of her eye. "I'd like to interview Simon Pembroke. Would it bother you if I did that?"

"No, it wouldn't bother me, but I don't know when you would catch him at the mill."

She tipped her head up. "Isn't he there every day?"

"He was. He's purchased more timber land, and he's out there supervising the forming of crews. He left me in charge."

Charity halted at the bottom of the porch steps. "Really? He gave you a promotion?"

"Is that so surprising?" He scowled at her, defensiveness in his voice.

"Oh no! I mean, you…I'm sure you can…it's just—"

Dale laughed out loud. "Did you know you squeak when you get flustered?"

Charity plunked her hands on her hips. "Dale Covington, are you trying to provoke me?"

He caught her hand and placed it back on his arm. "Simon promoted me to foreman because he needs someone to oversee the mill operation while he's out in the field."

Heat scorched her face. "That's wonderful, Dale. Truly. The reason I was surprised is because I know there are some who consider him a carpetbagger, and you're a Southerner. There is no animosity between you?"

They climbed the stairs and leaned against the porch

railing. "I suppose there was at first. But over the past few years we've put aside our differences."

"Did he say when he'd be back at the mill?"

"Probably not until next week."

Charity glanced at the boardinghouse window where a few of the boarders sat in the parlor. She didn't see Tate Ridley but couldn't help wondering how the man felt about Dale's promotion. She shivered.

Dale placed his hand on her back. "You better go inside. It's chilly out here."

"Thank you for a very special evening, Dale."

He gave a slow nod. "It was special for me, too." He walked her to the door and held it open. "Good night."

"Good night, Dale."

She climbed the stairs to her room and closed the door behind her, her head swirling with a half-dozen different emotions. She lit the lamp and sat with her elbows on the desk, her chin in her hands. She couldn't deny it. She was attracted to this man. How did that happen?

When she arrived here three and a half weeks ago, the drawl she heard in everyone's voice—Dale's included—sent shards of irritation through her. She'd wanted to blame every person she met for her father not coming home. The day she disembarked the carriage that brought her from Athens to Juniper Springs, she might have walked on the very soil where her father walked, where Wylie may have walked. The thought should have excited her, but that day she'd felt nothing but animosity. She'd thought her anger fueled her perseverance and gave her the motivation to press on. But now her anger and bitterness tumbled and twisted with empathy for Dale, compassion for those who'd lost so much, and even affection for a few of the folks she'd met. On top of everything, the flutters in her stomach every time she welcomed Dale into her thoughts mocked her with the paradox. How would she ever untangle the web?

"God help me. My feelings are so mixed up. I don't know how to balance what Dale told me about the slaves and how his attitudes have changed. I prepared myself to dislike him. Last Sunday and tonight he was such a different person from the day I first met him—gentler, caring. I don't know what to do."

Only God could sort out her bewildering emotions and put them in the right order. She closed her eyes and prayed. When she finished, she left her turmoil in God's hands.

She readied herself for bed, pulling on the heavier woolen socks and her warm flannel gown. She turned down the lamp and snuggled under the thick quilt Hannah had put on her bed.

Despite closing her eyes and curling up into a ball, sleep wouldn't come. She couldn't dismiss from her mind Dale's story of the black soldier who saved his life. Her chest tightened with emotion as she recalled Dale's telling of the way the man cared for his wounds and prayed for him. He was a slave, sent to fight in his master's place. He could have run off in the heat of battle, but he didn't. Instead, he asked for God's help in caring for a white man he didn't even know.

She breathed a prayer of gratitude for the black soldier and asked God to bless him. "I wonder if such a man might have tried to care for Father."

Dale blew out a frustrated breath. He'd begun inventorying this load of logs twice and lost count both times. A certain lady's face kept pulling his attention into a state of preoccupied distraction. The wistfulness in Charity's voice and the longing in her eyes when she spoke of her missing father wouldn't leave him alone. Their conversation on the back porch of the boardinghouse last Sunday afternoon echoed in his mind as well as the pained look on her face last night in response to his inquiry.

His own circumstances had haunted him for over six years, but at least he knew what happened. He steeled himself against the onslaught of horror crashing over him again. There was no wondering, no speculation. He'd repeatedly tried to put himself in her place, receiving word that her father had been wounded and captured, but then—nothing.

He moved back to the opposite side of the wagon and began counting and marking again. Eight at twelve feet. He scrawled the tally. Ten at eight feet, or was that eight at ten feet?

He and Charity had taken some sure steps toward friendship. How easy it was to tell her about the black soldier who saved his life. He'd never told anyone about that before. A niggling dissatisfaction nipped at him, however. Could he—should he justify forming a friendship with Charity Galbraith, that Yankee woman, as some in town called her? Was it wrong to feel comfortable in her presence and confide in her things he couldn't bring himself to voice to anyone else, not even Pastor Shuford?

Guilt skewered him. Wondering whether or not he should pursue a friendship with Charity wasn't what kept distracting him, and he knew it. As an officer in the Confederate army, he'd been privy to many confidential military files. He knew where the prisoner of war records were kept. Why didn't he share that information with her? Would she desire friendship with him if she knew?

Tate Ridley's words rolled through his mind again. *"A Yankee is a Yankee."* Dale ground his teeth, old hostilities slicing across his heart. His entire focus for over four years had been to destroy the enemy. In the aftermath of the war, the acid desire for reciprocation fueled the bitterness of his soul. Why should he care about Charity's pain? The Federals had inflicted plenty of pain on him. His life had been ravaged. His wounds left him crippled, his home and land stripped away. But his heart screamed when he thought about the one whose very soul mattered more than his own breath; if only he'd been given the chance to lay down his life in place of that one.

He sucked in a ragged breath and limped across the pole barn to sit on an overturned barrel. He wanted to roar out his pain. His heart pounded in his ears, and the familiar burning ache that started deep in his gut rose up to strangle him again. Pastor Shuford said it was bitterness that crippled him, not his wounds. For the first time, Dale realized what the preacher meant. A physical limp didn't make him a cripple, not in God's eyes. The debilitating impairment he dragged around with him was inside, bound by unseen shackles to which he'd clung for so long he wasn't sure how to peel his emotional fingers away.

With elbows on his knees, Dale dropped his head into his hands. "Oh, God, the war ended on this land over six years ago, but it still rages within me. I'm so tired of fighting. I hate the way this anger holds me captive."

"Let go, son. Let it go. Your hunger for revenge will devour you."

Dale raked his hands over his face. "But God, what they did—how do I let it go?"

"Give it to Me."

Letting go of his animosity toward those who took everything from him meant giving God control. Was he ready to do that? Could he take that step?

On the other side of the lumberyard, Tate Ridley and Jude Farley carried sawn boards from the mill and loaded them onto a wagon. The two made no pretense of their sentiments, openly spouting their hatred for everything connected with the North. In many ways they were more honest than Dale.

The way he'd looked forward to his evening with Charity last night proved it. The day she arrived and he'd first heard her speak, her Northern twang bayoneted him, and he hated her without even having been introduced. But the conversations he'd had with her over the past couple of weeks chipped away at the brittle rust around his heart. As he walked to the boardinghouse last night, his limp had all but disappeared in his anticipation of their time together. By the time they'd said good night, he could no longer deny he felt something for her. Was he a traitor, as Tate said? A few conversations didn't change who she was. He'd long equated the word *Yankee* with *enemy*. The two were synonymous.

But the Yankees he faced on the battlefield and his image of Charity weren't compatible. She wasn't a warrior. She was a daughter hoping to reconcile in her mind whatever destiny befell her father, and she was a friend seeking to ease the heartache of a mother.

A thought startled him. What if the black soldier who saved his life was this Wylie for whom Charity was searching? Unlikely, but possible, and a sudden urge to know the answer to that question burned within him.

He rose and walked back to the rack of logs. With the desire to help Charity find Wylie came another realization—another reason he'd refrained from telling her he had knowledge of the prisoner of war records. But this reason had been buried under an avalanche of resentment. Shoveling away the dross, he cleared the way to see his other purpose for keeping that information from her.

Whether he admitted it or not, the feelings he had for her went beyond empathy. If his suspicions were correct, learning the truth about what happened to her father would only deepen her pain, not relieve it. A stirring of protectiveness in his heart awakened a sense within him he thought was dead. Did that mean he was ready to break out of the bonds of bitterness?

In wrestling with the decision of whether or not friendship with Charity was right or wrong, a thread of dissatisfaction wormed through him. Friendship wasn't what he wanted.

Chapter 10

Dale braced himself for an argument. Tate crossed his arms and sneered in response to the instructions Dale just issued to the crew. A couple of the men resented Dale's new position as foreman, but no one more so than Tate Ridley.

Tate glanced to his left where Jude leaned against the side of the pole barn, whittling. "Seems to me you been dumpin' the heaviest work on me and the boys here while you been slackin' off ever since the boss's been away. He might've made you foreman since the both of you are Yankee-lovers, but it 'pears mighty lopsided, iffen you ask me."

Dale stared, unblinking, at Tate. "I didn't ask you. Nor do I intend to stand here wasting time explaining the number of orders on this clipboard or the time frame in which this crew of six men must complete these orders. I gave you and Jude and Amos your orders for the day. Since today is Saturday, you need to be finished by noon, or you'll stay until you are finished."

Amos hooted while Tate and Jude looked at each other. Tate took a step forward. "Maybe we'll just wait for Pembroke and see what he has to say."

"If you decide to do that, it'll be on your own time." Dale pulled the pencil from behind his ear. "I'm telling you for the last time, Tate. Get busy or go home."

Dale picked up the clipboard and propped one foot on the spoke of a wagon wheel. He made some notes on the side of one of the work orders while he waited to see what Tate and his cronies would do. When the trio stayed in place, Dale called out to one of the other men who worked closest to the office.

"Ned, go upstairs and see if you can find that Now Hiring sign on top of the file cabinet."

After some grumbling under their breaths, Tate and his buddies stomped off in the direction of the log rack. It wasn't the end of the matter, and Dale knew it.

Saturday being a short workday, Dale double-checked the work orders to make certain the most urgent ones would be completed and delivered on time. He went to help Zack and Ned with a load of siding boards. They finished the cutting and stacking in record time.

Dale dragged his sleeve across his forehead. "You fellows go ahead and start on that order of fence posts while I check on the other men." He skirted around the side of the building and came to the back of the pole barn. An ongoing exchange greeted him before he stepped into view of the three men.

"…oughta be an example to everyone in the county. It's a clear message."

Dale didn't feel like wasting time asking Tate what he meant. He rounded the corner. "How are you men coming? Need any help?"

Tate scoffed. "From you?" The other two men snickered.

Dale consulted the work order and checked their progress. "You only have another hour before the noon whistle sounds. You better get busy if you plan on leaving on time."

He turned on his heel and hitch-stepped back to help Zack and Ned with the fence posts.

The sawdust flew for the next hour, and by the time the shrill whistle blasted signifying quitting time, all the work was completed, checked off, and stacked. Dale handed out the pay envelopes, locked the office door, and made his way toward the general store where Clyde Sawyer was certain to have a number of orders to be delivered. When Dale told Clyde about his promotion, the merchant had rubbed his chin in consternation. But Dale didn't plan on quitting his second job at the store, much to Clyde's expressed relief. The more money he could sock away in the bank, the sooner he could become a landowner again.

He crossed the street in front of the post office. The town always bustled on Saturdays. Farm folk came to do their shopping and trading, along with socializing and gossiping. As Dale drew closer to the mercantile, animated conversations buzzed every few feet along the boardwalk. He couldn't catch enough to make sense of anything, but wide-eyed uneasiness on the faces around him and the foreboding tone in many voices set Dale's senses on alert. He didn't have the time or inclination to stop and chat, however, and he hastened to the back door of the mercantile.

Brisk business kept both Clyde and Betsy Sawyer busy waiting on customers out front. Since there were always extra deliveries on Saturday, Dale used Clyde's buckboard to speed up the process. Dale found the orders to be delivered hanging from a nail where Clyde always stuck them, and began loading the items into crates.

He went to the door that separated the storeroom from

the front. "Clyde, I'm taking six of these orders out. I should be back in an hour."

Clyde waved, and Dale hoisted the last loaded crate. As he shoved it onto the back of the buckboard, he couldn't help overhearing three men on the boardwalk.

"Lynched, I tell you. Right there by the side of the road where everyone can see."

"You don't say."

"I hear tell they stuck a cross in the ground right beside the tree they hung him from, and don't ya know, they set fire to that there cross."

Another man shook his head. "Ain't been any lynchin's around these parts since back in '64."

"Ain't the same. This one was a darkie."

The blood coursing through Dale's veins froze. He limped over to the men.

"What's this about a lynching?"

One of the men thumbed his suspender. "Yup, hanged him there from a big oak tree for everybody to see. Burned a cross beside him, too."

Was this what Tate and the others were talking about? "Where was this?"

"Over by the Athens road." The old timer scratched his head. "Not far from the river."

Dread oozed through Dale's being. His sister and her husband lived out that way. Pastor Shuford urged him numerous times to bury the hatchet, reminding him that Auralie was all the family he had left. If there was anything of which he needed no reminding, it was that his family was gone.

Auralie and Colton had a black man, Barnabas, who worked for them. Dale had never told them so, but he was secretly glad Barnabas stayed on the place protecting his sister and her baby while her husband was off fighting.

When the war ended, the conflict between him and Auralie seemed too wide to bridge. The reasons seemed ridiculously petty now.

Every direction Dale turned Sunday morning, talk of the lynching raged like wildfire. It hardly seemed appropriate conversation between worshippers entering the house of God, but the event had sent a shock wave through the town, and everyone had an opinion. Speculation and accusations galloped faster than a runaway horse heading for the barn. Every snippet of conversation that reached Dale's ear sent a blade of regret slicing deeper into his conscience.

All afternoon the day before, Dale made his deliveries for Clyde Sawyer and repeatedly ran into people adding more gruesome details to an already horrendous story. The lynching remained on the lips of every person in town this morning. Dale carried enough grisly memories of the war with him. He didn't need or want to paint a picture in his head of the unholy activities that took place out on the Athens road two nights ago.

Dale hung back from the groups of people gathering in the churchyard. He saw Charity walking toward the church with Hannah and the Ferguson ladies, but the unsettled state of his emotions this morning left him in no mood to talk to anyone. If Charity asked him what he thought about it, he had no answer. He couldn't put into words the turmoil that churned through him, and he had no desire to participate in any of the conversations circulating through the crowd. Instead, he stepped back into the shadows and kept watching down the road as wagons and carriages arrived for the Sunday morning services. When the church bell rang, everyone made their way inside. Everyone except Dale.

The opening hymn drifted through the closed doors, but

Dale lingered outside, hoping to greet Auralie and Colton when they arrived. He'd tossed and turned the entire night. If only he'd put his animosity aside when Pastor Shuford encouraged him to do so. He kicked a clod of dirt, watching it burst apart and scatter. He'd wasted so much time fostering his rancor and at the same time feeding his self-pity, privately envying those people who had family. He'd told himself he was alone, no family left, but that wasn't true. Indignant anger took control of him when Auralie announced her marriage to Colton. Shame filled him when he remembered telling her she was no longer his sister.

The memory poured hot coals of remorse over him. Pastor Shuford was right. Refusing to reconcile with Auralie had robbed both of them of the joys of family.

The congregation finished the first hymn and began singing a second, and Auralie and Colton had still not appeared. They rarely missed church, even with their two little ones. Auralie and Colton had repeatedly told him they'd been praying for him and hoped he'd choose to be part of their family, but he'd refused. He raked his hands through his hair. He didn't have family because he'd turned his back on them. What a fool he'd been. He'd been a fool about a lot of things. He looked up the road again, but no wagon appeared around the bend.

With his head in his hands, Dale wondered for the thousandth time why the black soldier bothered to save his life. Dale had seen the scars on the man's back when he took his shirt off and used it to bind Dale's wounds. How could a man who'd been beaten and forced into slavery by white men, sent to fight in a war that could have resulted in continued slavery if the South had won, show such compassion for a white man?

"God, why did he do that? *How* could he do that?"

There was only one way—the way Pastor Shuford had

been telling him for six years. The only way he would ever reconcile with Auralie, or understand what motivated that soldier to do what he did, or break free of the invisible shackles that bound him was by letting God have control. He pressed his lips tightly together. Could he find the courage to take such a step?

He blew out a stiff breath and looked for Auralie and Colton's wagon one more time. Clearly, they weren't coming to church this morning, and Dale feared the reason. He rose and walked as fast as his limp would allow down the street to the livery to borrow a horse. He had to ride out there. He had to know. He had to tell Auralie how sorry he was and ask her and Colton to forgive him.

As he walked, he lifted his voice to heaven. "God, I pray that Barnabas is all right, but somebody somewhere is grieving for the man who was lynched. I've been so stiff-necked and hard-hearted, Lord. Please forgive me."

When he reached the stable, the hostler told him to pick out a mount and saddle it himself. Dale pulled a gelding from his stall and tossed a saddle on his back. The horse snorted in protest at being taken away from his feed bin. Dale patted his neck.

"Sorry, fella, but this is one mission I don't intend to fail."

Charity peeked from the corner of her eye during the singing to see if Dale had come in. She'd seen him in church the first three Sundays that she'd been in Juniper Springs. A prick of concern poked her, but she immediately dismissed it. There were a dozen possible reasons he wasn't there. But of all Sundays for him to miss, why this one?

After hearing the dreadful news about the black man they'd found hanging beside a burned cross, Charity wanted—no, she needed—to talk to Dale more than ever. She simply couldn't comprehend such a vile act. Could he?

In the light of the lynching, Dale's warnings to be careful rang in her head. At the time, she couldn't imagine anyone taking out their resentment of her as a Yankee in any way other than a frown and a snub. Now she wasn't so sure. But she couldn't quit, not now.

She still had her articles to write, and what she'd learned since coming here shed a whole new light on the slant of her stories. Her editor expected the first article on his desk before the end of October, and she'd not disappoint him.

But her dogged determination sent agitation swirling through her stomach. She was no closer to finding Wylie or learning what became of her father than she was when she first arrived. Every person with whom she'd spoken, every place she looked, she kept running into dead ends. The tenacity that drove her made the nerve endings in her scalp tingle. She *would not* give up.

The preacher's voice rose and fell with emotion as he grasped the sides of the pulpit and leaned forward. "The news of this lynching is on everyone's lips, but I wonder how many of those talking about it view it as a tragedy— just as tragic as the war. For four and a half years the destruction and the death toll made us gasp. It was more than we could comprehend."

He pounded his fist on the pulpit. "Well, I say that the lynching of this man is every bit as wicked and depraved as any of the atrocities of war, maybe even more so."

Charity blinked and held her breath. Since yesterday, she'd tried not to think about the unspeakable possibility of the murdered man being Wylie. Another wave of nausea crashed over her, and she bit her lip.

The pastor moved to the side of the pulpit and stepped down from the platform, walked down the aisle, beseeching the people to listen. "Don't you see? In a war, we're told there is an enemy who means us harm, and the soldiers go out and put their lives in danger to protect their homeland from that enemy."

He backed up slowly, turning from side to side and looking into the faces of those seated on the wooden benches. "That man who was hung wasn't an enemy. He didn't mean anyone any harm. The soldiers weren't called up to go out and hunt him down. The men who committed this ungodly act didn't put their own lives in danger. In fact, they hid behind hooded masks like cowards!" With every declaration, the volume and intensity of the preacher's voice increased until he was shouting.

A trembling began in the pit of Charity's stomach. The preacher was declaring the same sentiments she felt. Tears pricked her eyes.

"God's Word instructs us to put away malice, and he who sheds innocent blood will himself be condemned."

Charity poised on the edge of the bench, every muscle tensed in anticipation.

The pastor stood facing the silent congregation with his arms stretched out to his side like a loving parent encouraging his children to come. "Hasn't there been enough death? The animosity must cease." His voice broke as he began to weep. "Search your hearts. Put away the hatred. Let go of the bitterness and its poison."

His voice fell to almost a whisper, and Charity had to strain to hear him.

"And what do you put in the place of that hatred?" He turned his palms up and held his arms out. "Forgiveness, my friends. Yes, I can see in the eyes of many here this morning that you think I'm asking too much of you. But I'm not the one doing the asking." He held up his Bible. "God is."

Charity squirmed in her seat. How could she forgive the people who took her father from her?

With tears streaming down his face, Pastor Shuford's next words arrested her heart.

"Jesus said, 'Father, forgive them; for they know not what they do.' "

Brokenness rendered her weak with guilt and regret.

Precious Lord Jesus, help me forgive.

Chapter 11

Humbling himself never came easy for Dale, and finding the words to express a heartfelt apology tested his resolve, but God birthed a seed of fortitude within him and smoothed the way. The expression on Auralie's face when she opened the door to his knock would linger with Dale for as long as he drew breath. Relying on God's strength to carry out his purpose, Dale tasted the sweetness of His promise when he embraced his sister and shook his brother-in-law's hand.

Learning that their reason for missing church had nothing to do with Barnabas rendered Dale weak with relief. Both of the children were down with the croup. A slight moan shuddered through him at the sound of their coughing, but the little ones would be fine in a few days.

His private meeting with Barnabas had started out awkwardly, but he managed to tell the man how much it meant to him, knowing his sister wasn't alone during those awful months. Expressing his thanks to the former slave felt odd, to be sure, but his heart smiled when Barnabas got over the shock and finally responded with upturned lips and a slight nod of his head.

Despite the shortness of the visit, Dale savored the reconciliation with his sister. Auralie had urged him to stay for dinner, but he'd begged off, promising to return another day. Dale reined the gelding around and raised his hand in farewell. Auralie stood beside her husband on the front porch, waving and wiping tears away.

He nudged the horse into a canter down the road. The sun climbed above the treetops, chasing the morning chill into hiding as Dale headed back to town. Gratefulness hung around his shoulders like a cloak with the assurance of the restored family connection, but a dark cloud followed him. The lynching drew a sinister curtain around the community, and Dale's concern for Charity grew. Even though he'd already warned Tate and his friends to leave her alone, in light of the news on everyone's lips, he couldn't be sure of her safety. Perhaps it was time for another talk with her.

When he passed the sign that proclaimed Welcome to Juniper Springs, he left the horse at the livery, paid his twenty-five cents for the loan of the animal, and turned his feet in the direction of the boardinghouse. He let himself in through the white picket gate in the front, but before he reached the porch steps, he spied Charity in the side yard, sitting on a small garden bench amid a swirl of autumn leaves.

He rounded the corner of the house, and she looked up. The scowl around her eyes immediately softened, and she rose to greet him.

"I looked for you in church this morning."

"There was something I had to do." Dale gestured toward the back porch. "Can we sit back here where we can talk?"

They climbed the three steps to the back porch, and Dale noticed the wicker chairs that had mysteriously disappeared last Sunday were back in place. He smothered a tiny chuckle. Hannah Sparrow had a mischievous streak.

The chairs offered to put distance between him and Charity, but today he had a choice. He crossed to the swing.

"Shall we?"

Despite the small smile that graced Charity's lips, unease creased her brow. A momentary question stung him. Was her angst due to the word around town of the lynching, or did the prospect of sitting close to him cause her discomfort?

She gathered her shawl around her and settled onto the swing. He lowered himself beside her, turning slightly to face her.

"I'm sure you've heard what happened." Distress laced her voice. "The whole town is talking about it."

Dale nodded. "Yes. That's why I wanted to talk with you."

She interlaced her fingers and clung to the corners of her shawl until her knuckles were white. A visible shiver coursed through her, but Dale suspected she wasn't chilled.

"How can anyone do such a horrible thing, Dale?"

Painful memories lanced him. "Thousands of horrible things were committed in the name of war for over four years."

She clutched his arm. "But the war is over. Like the preacher said this morning, that man didn't mean anyone any harm." She shook her head. "I don't understand the mentality of a person who could do something like that. One of the things I'm trying to clarify for my articles is the attitudes and opinions of people, and how they affect the Reconstruction."

Dale frowned. "I'd hoped you would write with a more positive slant. Not everyone in the South is as ignorant as the ones who hung that man."

She shot back a retort. "I know that." She released a sigh. "I'm sorry. I didn't mean to snap at you. This is obviously not your fault, but it's stirred some very powerful feelings in a lot of people."

He pressed his lips together tightly. He hoped she'd not take exception to what he needed to say. "My point exactly. Charity, whoever did this isn't likely to be put off by the fact that you're a woman." The words he overheard Tate say at the sawmill echoed in his mind.

"...oughta be an example to everyone in the county. The message is clear."

A cold chill gripped him, followed in its wake by anger. But this anger was different from the heavy burden he'd dragged around for years. His gaze traced the outline of the stubborn set of her jaw.

"Why hasn't the sheriff done anything?" She leaned closer and dropped the volume of her voice. "I think Tate Ridley knows something about it. You should have seen the smug look on his face at dinner today."

He worked to keep his tone quiet and calming. "Miles Flint can't arrest anyone for the crime until he has solid proof. Tate said he was playing cards Friday night, and his friends are backing up his story. Unfortunately, a smug look on his face isn't enough to build a case against the man."

A tiny growl of frustration emerged from her lips. "You sound just like the rest of them. Dale, a horrible crime has been committed, and all anyone is doing about it is talking."

She rose from the swing and paced the length of the

porch and returned. He let her spout her vexation. She stopped and extended her arms, palms up in entreaty.

"Did this man have family? Will they know what happened to him? What if no one is ever punished for his murder?" Her voice broke, and she covered her face with her hands. Her muffled words defined her dread. "Dale, what if that man was Wylie? How could I ever tell Essie that her son—"

Dale fairly leaped from the swing and was at her side in two strides. He captured her wrists and gave them a gentle tug. "Charity, I've asked myself those very same questions, and I agree with you. It *was* a horrible crime. Hatred is so deeply ingrained in some people they can't see past it." He cupped her chin and tipped her face up. "You and I can't change what happened—not the murder two nights ago, and not the death and destruction of war. All we can control is the way we respond to it."

She drew in a deep breath and let it out slowly. "I know."

He cocked his head at her. "I don't suppose you'd listen if I asked you to discontinue your search."

She arched an eyebrow and set her jaw in a stubborn posture that was becoming familiar.

He wanted to argue with her but knew it to be futile. "I didn't think so."

She adjusted her shawl and returned to the swing. "I looked for you this morning in church. When you weren't there, I grew concerned."

Dale sat beside her. "I went out to visit my sister and brother-in-law. There was something I needed to do that I'd put off far too long."

Charity stood and pushed back the desk chair. Stretching her stiff legs felt good. Trying to put articles together to please Mr. Peabody and the readership of the *Keystone* put every journalistic skill she had to the test. Nothing she'd written this morning rang true. Just when she knew the angle with which she wanted to address these articles, the news of the lynching set her off balance. Perhaps she needed a brisk walk in the crisp fall air to clear her head.

She grabbed her shawl and hurried down the stairs. She found Hannah rattling around in the kitchen.

"I'm going for a walk. Is there anything you need from the store?"

"Oh yes." Hannah wiped her hands on her apron. "You would save me a trip if you could pick up a couple of fat stewing hens at the butcher." She stepped over to a shelf in the corner and pulled down a crock. She withdrew a few coins and deposited them into Charity's hand. "That should cover it. Be sure to get some nice plump ones."

Charity slipped the coins into her reticule. "I won't be long." She stepped out the back door and breathed deeply of the spicy scent of autumn leaves and wood smoke. A squirrel scolded her for interrupting his acorn-gathering. She grinned at him.

"All right, I'm leaving." The leaf-strewn pathway around the side of the house crunched beneath her feet.

She crossed the street and set out down the boardwalk. She smiled and said hello to several people she recognized from seeing them in church. Some returned the greeting while others narrowed their eyes in suspicion and passed by without so much as a nod.

The bell over the door of the butcher sang cheerfully as she entered. A stout man in a soiled apron gave her a gap-toothed smile.

"*Vat es* do you need today, *Fräulein*?" His German accent tickled her ears after hearing so much Southern dialect over the past month.

"Mrs. Sparrow at the boardinghouse wants two plump

stewing hens." She dug Hannah's money from her reticule and held it out to the man. He bobbed his head and deposited the coins. She waited while he wrapped the birds in paper.

With the promise of Hannah's chicken and dumplings in her arms, Charity headed back to the boardinghouse. As she passed by the saloon, two men nearly collided with her as they exited.

"Well now, who do we have here?" One of the men blocked her way.

"This here is that Yankee writer lady. Wonder what all she's writin' 'bout us poor ign'rant Southern folks."

Charity sucked in a breath and clutched the chickens tighter. She attempted to step around the men, but they bumped her into the alley between the saloon and the hotel. One of the men grabbed her wrist, causing her to drop the hens in the dirt. He leaned close and hissed in her face.

"You best watch your step if you know what's good for you."

The second man, who looked vaguely familiar, took up where the first one left off. Both men reeked of sour mash whiskey. "You keep askin' a lot of nosy questions about things that don't concern you, maybe you'll find yourself up to your neck in more trouble than you bargained for, missy."

Charity's heart pounded, but she refused to cower. She lifted her chin and drew herself up as tall as she could. "Take your hands off me. How dare you threaten me? You two are nothing but unprincipled reprobates with nothing better to do than harass a woman." She yanked her wrist free. "Furthermore, I suspect that you likely had something to do with murdering that poor man last week, and I hope you get everything that's coming to you."

The first man hooted in derision. "Whoever done that was just clearin' out the vermin."

Charity's lungs heaved with indignation. "I'm sure the sheriff will be very interested in your opinion."

The second man snarled and grasped her upper arm in a vise grip, digging his fingers into her flesh until she winced. His breath turned her stomach. "You better not go makin' any accusations you can't prove."

Before she could swing her foot back to give the bully a hard kick, Dale stomped across the boardwalk and knocked the man on his backside. Had the situation not been so tense, she'd have thrown her arms around his neck.

Dale glared down at the man lying in the dirt between two rubbish cans and pointed his finger in the heathen's face. "You're lucky I can control my temper." He kicked the man's leg. "Get up."

He jerked his gaze to Jude Farley standing a few feet away. "Jude, I warned you and the others at the sawmill to leave Miss Galbraith alone. Now I'm telling you, if you even look at her sideways, you'll have me to deal with. You understand?"

Jude muttered under his breath.

Dale eyed the first man who dusted off his trousers. "What's your name?"

The stranger sneered. "None of your business."

Dale nodded. "That's all right, you don't have to tell me, because I'm making it my business to find out."

He turned to Charity whose expression was a mixture of outrage and cussed stubbornness. "Are you all right?"

She answered through gritted teeth. "I'm fine."

Two chickens lay at Charity's feet, unrolled from their paper wrapping and now coated with dirt. He pointed at the two hapless birds. "How much did these cost?"

Charity told him, and he held his palm out to the men. "Pay up."

Both men dug in their pockets and tossed a few coins in Dale's hand. He in turn handed the money to Charity. She gave the pair of miscreants one last glare before turning on her heel and marching down the boardwalk toward the butcher.

Dale backed the two weasels up against the wall. "If you ever touch Miss Galbraith again, I will personally drag what's left of you to the sheriff's office and throw your worthless hides in jail."

The two skulked away, muttering oaths. Dale clenched his fists as he watched them go, trying to control his rage at seeing Charity accosted.

She returned a few minutes later with a bundle wrapped in butcher paper. Dale relieved her of the package. "I'll walk you home."

"Thank you, Dale. Those two made me so mad, but I wasn't any match for them."

His anger fought for expression, but he held it in check. "What did they say to you?"

"Nothing too much. They just don't like the fact that I'm a Yankee and I'm writing about the Reconstruction."

He shot a glance her way. Why did he feel she wasn't telling him everything?

"I didn't know that one man, but I'll deal with Jude at the sawmill." He paused. "You will tell me if anyone bothers you again, won't you."

She slipped her hand through the crook of his elbow. "I'm sure they won't."

"Charity…"

She pointed to a boy tacking up a notice on a post. "What's that?"

They stopped to read the poster over the boy's shoulder. The young towheaded fellow looked up at them. "Preacher is payin' me fifteen cents to hang these all over town."

Dale grinned down at him. "Fifteen cents? That'll buy a lot of candy."

The youngster grinned back. "I'm partial to peppermint." He tipped his cap to Charity. "I best get goin'. I got work to do."

Charity read the large headline aloud. "A Unity Rally?"

The notice proclaimed that Pastor Shuford called for everyone in town to attend church this upcoming Sunday because he was going to set forth a challenge to every person to put aside their malice and take a stand against the recent violence and come together in unity.

A tiny scowl dipped Charity's brow. "I'm glad somebody is doing something."

Dale released a soft snort. "Miles Flint better be there because things are likely to get pretty heated."

They continued to the boardinghouse. Dale handed Charity the paper-wrapped package and opened the door for her. "Charity, may I escort you to church this Sunday?"

She cocked her head. "Yes, you may."

He managed a tight smile and bid her a good afternoon. His temper still simmered as he walked to the mercantile. What was he thinking? Was it possible for a Yankee and a Rebel to worship together?

A smirk tilted his mouth. "I suppose we'll find out."

Chapter 12

The little church filled quickly, and Charity was glad Dale suggested they arrive early. Men stood to give ladies their seats, and by the time Pastor Shuford led in the singing of "Guide Me, O Thou Great Jehovah," the chapel was packed. As the hymn died away and people settled in, the preacher began by asking those who had lost someone in the war to raise their hands.

Charity turned in her seat and swept a glance across the room. Almost every hand went up. The pastor walked up and down the center aisle counting. He began whittling down the focus with more specific questions, demonstrating how some had lost sons or fathers, brothers or cousins, husbands or sweethearts. Some lost multiple loved ones, while others admitted to nightmares or periods of melancholia. Some lost land or business or fortune.

People all over the room murmured in response. A muffled sob sounded from the far right while others cleared their throats, fighting off tears.

Pastor Shuford returned to the front and held his arms out wide. "Do you see what we've shown here this morning? From the looks of it, almost the entire town is here today, and there isn't a person in this room who hasn't lost someone or something. True, some have lost more than others, but that should only serve to encourage us to be more compassionate, more Christlike."

Charity leaned slightly forward in her seat, hanging on every word. The picture he so eloquently painted was exactly the portrait she'd been trying to capture in her articles—this war affected everyone.

"Most of the folks here are Southern-born." The preacher cast his hand in a wide, encompassing arc. "But not all."

A hush fell over the crowd. Charity lowered her gaze to her lap. She'd experienced enough disdain over the past month to know several in the congregation stared at her. Hadn't the preacher shown, though, that everyone had suffered loss?

He stepped up onto the platform, and his booming voice carried to every corner. "South or North. Rich or poor. Learned or illiterate. Man or woman. Free or bond." He lowered his voice and sent a hard look across the packed pews. "And yes, white or black." He opened his Bible.

"In the tenth chapter of Acts, the apostle Peter preached that God is no respecter of persons. Brothers and sisters, listen to me. *Every* man who loves and fears God is himself a work of righteousness, because our Lord and Savior Jesus Christ is Lord of ALL!"

A man leaped to his feet two rows in front of Charity and Dale.

"That ain't so, preacher. Ain't no colored equal to a white man."

The preacher held his Bible aloft. "These aren't my words, Floyd. This is God's Word." He gestured to all assembled. "And Juniper Springs is a community. You and your family are part of this community, just like every other person in this room."

Another man stood. "I don't see no coloreds in this room."

A few others called out their agreement in ugly terms unfit for women and children's ears.

"Friends, please." Pastor Shuford held up his hands. "We must come together. Half of the word *community* is 'unity.' Violence has no place here. If we are to live as children of God, then we must acknowledge that we are *all* a family."

Two men toward the rear began arguing, and Charity tucked her bottom lip between her teeth. Squabbling only served to widen the gap separating the different persuasions. Above the angry shouts, the preacher's pleading voice called for attention.

"Listen to what God says. 'God so loved the *world*, that he gave his only begotten Son, that *whosoever* believeth in him should not perish, but have everlasting life.' Friends, neighbors, I tell you, the persecution and acts of violence are an abomination in God's eyes."

"What about violence done against us, preacher?"

"Them darkies is to blame. It's 'cause of them that war came down on us."

"Oh hush, Jess. You don't know what you're talking about."

A couple of women rose and ushered their children out the door.

Dale bent his head low and muttered. "This isn't right. God, help me." He stood and held up his hand for quiet.

Charity caught her breath, and her pulse tripped faster. She raised her eyes to the determined set to his jaw.

"Most of you here know me. You know who I am and what I was before the war. My family was wealthy and powerful. Now I work at the sawmill and the general store."

Comments buzzed all around them, but Dale didn't appear affected by anyone's opinions. He spoke up with confidence and conviction.

"I want to tell you about a man I met during the war. I'd been wounded—in my side and my leg. I tried to crawl for cover, but I couldn't move. Artillery exploded all around me. Rifle fire whistled on every side. I was a doomed man."

Tears burned Charity's eyes, and her throat tightened. She prayed silently for God's strength for Dale to say what needed to be said, and for those around to listen, not just with their ears but with their hearts.

"A man I did not know crawled over to me and told me I was going to be all right. He carried me into the woods, and hid me where I'd be safe until the battle was over. Then he tore his own shirt to wrap around my wounds. He gave me water and took care of me. When it was safe to move, he carried me. For two days we traveled until he brought me to a regiment that had a doctor. All during that time, this man prayed for me. He prayed for strength to carry me, and he prayed for God to let me live."

Charity dabbed tears from her eyes and glanced around the room. Every face turned toward Dale, every eye riveted on him.

"This man put his own life in danger to save me. He didn't have to do that. He didn't even know me. But he knew Someone else. He knew Jesus. I could tell by the way he kept up a continuous conversation, not with me, but with the Lord."

Dale shook his head and his voice broke. "I've asked myself a thousand times why that man did what he did. There is only one answer. He let Jesus do it through him."

The man two rows ahead spoke up. "I suppose you're gonna tell us he was a Yankee."

Dale turned his head. "No, Floyd. He wasn't a Yankee. He was a slave."

A gasp rippled through the crowd. Dale sat down, and Charity risked a sideways glance at him. How hard was it for a once-wealthy, influential man to stand before the town and relate the story he'd hidden in his heart for six years?

Pastor Shuford stepped down from the platform. "Dale, did you tell this man you couldn't accept his help because he was black?"

Dale shook his head. "No, sir."

The preacher scanned the room. "It's a good thing God isn't bigoted against sinners, for we'd surely all be as doomed as Dale was on that battlefield. Had it not been for the compassion shown by that man, Dale wouldn't be here today to tell us about it." He gestured toward Dale. "When a man acts in a Christlike way, does God ask about the color of his skin to determine whether or not the act is acceptable in His sight?"

A handful of men stood and made some uncouth remarks, walking out one after the other. Charity recognized two as the ones who'd accosted her in the alley.

Weariness evidenced itself in the preacher's voice and face as he addressed those remaining. "Brothers and sisters, instead of a closing hymn, I'd like for us to have a time of silent prayer, and each of us search our hearts for those prejudices God would have us remove."

Heads bowed and peace reigned. As each one finished praying, feet shuffled and hushed whispers accompanied them as people quietly got up and left. Charity raised her head to find Dale watching her. He rose and held out his hand.

She placed her fingers within the safety of his grasp and joined him tiptoeing out of the church.

Pastor Shuford stood by the door. "Thank you for what you said, Dale. You never told me that before."

Charity peered up and watched Dale's jaw twitch. She doubted that she'd ever know how much his speech cost him.

Low, gray clouds hung above the treetops and swallowed the sun as Dale walked her to the boardinghouse in silence, his limp barely perceptible. A chilly breeze shook leaves loose from their tethers and blew them across the road, tumbling with the ones that had fallen before them. No matter how long the leaves clung to the branches, eventually they'd all join the seasonal dance in a patchwork of colors.

They climbed the porch steps at the boardinghouse, and Dale reached for the door. Charity put out her hand to stop him. "I really admire what you did today. Relating your experience in front of everybody, especially those you knew would scorn it, took great fortitude."

His lips pressed together, and he lowered his gaze. "I'm not the man I once was."

She touched his hand. "No, you aren't. You're better."

Charity crumpled another sheet of paper and tossed it in the corner with the rest. She propped her elbows on the desk and laid her head in her hands. Not a single attempt at writing the first article satisfied her. She stood and paced the small bedroom between the door and the single window, muttering to herself.

"Something's missing." Agitation climbed her frame as she glared at the pile of discarded beginnings of her writing. "It lacks cohesiveness." She crossed to the window and pushed the filmy white curtain aside with her fingertips. "How do I capture what I can't define?"

A folded piece of paper taunted her from the corner of the desk. She picked up the telegram and opened it, even though she could quote it word for word.

Must have first article by Nov 1.

That was it. No wasted words. But she read between the brevity and the signature. If she couldn't produce the first article on time, she might as well not bother writing the rest, and she couldn't afford to lose this assignment.

She slid one finger over her lips and contemplated informing Mr. Peabody of her two other missions. Couldn't she tie a search for a former slave and a Union officer into her other articles? Her editor might find it intriguing enough to warrant an additional article and grant her more time. On the other hand, catering to the readership was always foremost in the man's mind. No doubt he'd remind her that the people of prominence and affluence who subscribed to *Keystone* likely wouldn't be interested in a lowly dressmaker wanting to reunite with her long lost son.

She returned to the desk and pulled out a fresh sheet of paper, its vast emptiness looming before her. In order to keep her job, she had to draw a portrait with words in a way to captivate her audience. The trouble was the issues that captivated her were very different from the ones that would appeal to a Northern aristocrat.

Frost sugarcoated the ground when Dale stepped out the door of his house. He pulled his collar up around his ears and thrust his hands into his pockets. Dawn had barely broken, and he didn't know if the Ferguson ladies' bakery would be open yet, but he figured if he tapped on the door, they'd let him in.

His boots crunched through the leaves as the town

awoke around him. A rooster crowed, a dog barked, the aroma of fresh coffee boiling on somebody's stove tantalized his senses, and muted sunlight filtered through the trees along the top of the mountain east of town.

He'd been awake for hours, unsettled thoughts causing sleep to remain out of his reach. People still talked of the lynching, but the past two days, the topic of most conversations was Pastor Shuford's unorthodox church service. Many folks stated adamantly that they never intended to forget or forgive. Others revealed hearts laced with bigotry. Had it not been for God sending that black soldier to save his life, he feared he'd be among them. He couldn't expect people to see things from his point of view if they hadn't experienced what he had. Still, he prayed a work of grace to be done within those who still viewed the former slaves the way Tate Ridley did.

Margaret Ferguson was just unlocking the front door of the bakery when Dale arrived. She gave him a syrupy smile while she wrapped up the apple fritters he selected, and batted her eyelashes at him when he paid her and bid her a polite good morning.

As soon as he left the bakery, his thoughts returned to those ponderings that had kept him awake most of the night. The "brotherhood," as Tate Ridley referred to it, tended to protect each other, so Dale wasn't surprised that some of Tate's cronies swore they'd all been playing cards the night the man was lynched. Tate's suggestion that perhaps Dale should join them, coupled with the comments he overheard, weren't enough to make an accusation, but they certainly raised Dale's suspicions.

Smoke curled from the stovepipe emerging from the sawmill office when Dale crossed the bridge. Hopefully Simon had brewed a fresh pot of coffee rather than warming up yesterday's leftovers. When Dale walked in, Simon looked over his shoulder at him. "You're early."

Dale shrugged. "Couldn't sleep. Figured I might as well get an early start." He laid one of the apple fritters on Simon's desk. "Brought you some breakfast."

"Thanks."

Dale poured two cups of coffee and handed one to Simon.

Simon took a noisy slurp. "I'm real pleased with the way you've kept things going here while I was at the logging camp."

Dale gave him a nod of appreciation.

"I'm leaving for the camp again today. Should be back early next week." Simon took a bite of his fritter. "But there's something I wanted to talk to you about." .

Simon's tone caught Dale's attention. "Something wrong?"

"Not sure." Simon took another slurp of coffee. "In the light of what happened a week and a half ago, I'd like you to keep an extra close eye on Tate." Simon shook his head. "That one's a troublemaker. I hope I'm wrong, but I think he might have had something to do with that lynching."

Dale shot a hard look at his boss. He hadn't said anything Dale didn't already suspect, but he wanted to know why Simon thought so.

Dale sat across from Simon. "I've heard a few things he's said. A few weeks ago he suggested I attend a meeting of their brotherhood—that's what he called it, but you and I both know who they are."

"Hmph. The Klan. I thought as much." Simon finished off his fritter and licked his fingers. "I was coming back from the logging camp that Friday. It was getting late, and I knew I'd never make it before nightfall, so I made camp in the woods out by the Athens road. I'd already turned in when I heard voices. Three or four men. Couldn't really see them, but one of them was Tate. I recognized his voice."

"Did you hear what they said?"

"Just bits and pieces. There was a wind blowing that night. That's why I didn't keep the campfire going."

Dale set his coffee mug down and waited for Simon to go on.

"I heard something that sounded like, 'He ain't gonna have no more need of it,' or something like that. They moved on pretty quick."

"They didn't see you?"

Simon shook his head. "Don't think so."

Dale rubbed his hand across his face. "Have you talked to Miles Flint about this?"

"No. There's enough hard feelings around here toward anyone from the North. Didn't figure the word of a Yankee would be worth much."

Dale finished off his coffee. "There are some who don't think my word is worth much either."

Chapter 13

Charity stepped back to allow a young mother with two children to enter the general store ahead of her. The little ones, a girl and a boy, looked enough alike to be twins, but the difference in their height indicated the girl was a couple of years older. Before they were a half-dozen steps inside the store, the little boy dashed to the glass case that displayed the candy.

Saturday morning business was brisk, and Charity scooted past a few folks to pick up another package of writing paper. A wave of guilt pricked her when she thought of the number of sheets she'd wasted, but this time she knew exactly what she was going to write. At least, she hoped she knew.

She moved toward the counter and found herself standing behind the young mother again. Listening to the children's chatter brought a smile to Charity's heart. She'd hoped to have a family one day, but most men didn't want a woman who had a career.

The little boy turned around and peered up at her. "Hi, lady. Whatcha buyin'?"

His mother gave his shoulder a gentle tap. "Timothy! That's not polite." She turned and gave Charity an apologetic look. "I'm sorry. He just says whatever is on his mind."

Charity smiled. "It's all right. Both of your children are adorable."

The woman blushed. "Thank you. We haven't been introduced, but I've seen you at church. I'm Auralie Danfield, and this is my daughter, Rose, and my son, Timothy."

"Papa hadta go to the freight depot," Timothy piped up. "He said he'd be back in two shakes of a lamb's tail."

Charity chuckled, and Auralie placed her hand atop Timothy's head. "You're Miss Galbraith, aren't you? My brother mentioned you were here on assignment from your magazine."

"Your brother?"

"Dale Covington is my brother."

Charity nodded with understanding. "I should have seen the resemblance. Dale told me he had a sister, and I do recall seeing you and your family in church, but I didn't make the connection. It's nice to meet you."

The storekeeper finished Mrs. Danfield's order, and she stepped aside so Charity could pay for her paper. She sneaked a peek at the children, both of whom had their noses pressed against the glass case, gazing with longing at the selection of candy. Charity leaned toward their mother and whispered. "May they each have a peppermint stick?"

Her new friend smiled and nodded. "I suppose one peppermint stick won't spoil them too badly."

Rose and Timothy chorused a "thank you, ma'am"

and scampered outside with their treat, while Charity became better acquainted with Dale's sister. The two women strolled out to the boardwalk together. The previous day's chill had mellowed into a milder, sunny day, providing a pleasant moment for visiting while they waited for Mr. Danfield to return for his family.

"I'm glad I finally got to meet you, Miss Galbraith."

"Please, call me Charity."

"Only if you will call me Auralie." She set her market basket down and turned to check on the children before continuing. "Are you going to write about last Sunday's church service in your articles?"

Charity tilted her head. "I hope to include many angles in the articles, but I must admit last Sunday's service was different."

Auralie's eyes misted. "I didn't know about that black soldier who saved my brother's life."

"Dale said he hadn't told people about that, but why didn't he tell you?"

Tiny lines appeared between Auralie's brows. "Dale and I have been estranged for the past ten years. He didn't approve of me marrying Colton. When the war started and Colton fought for the North, Dale was outraged. He refused to have anything to do with us. He even made it clear that we weren't welcome at his wedding."

"His—" Charity's breath caught. "His wedding? I didn't know he was married."

"Oh dear. Perhaps I shouldn't have said anything." Auralie touched her lips with her fingertips. "My brother has always guarded his privacy, but I didn't realize he'd not told you he'd been married."

The revelation spun in Charity's mind. "I don't believe I've seen his wife."

"Oh no." Auralie shook her head. "She died six years ago."

"I see." Uncertainty rattled her. Perhaps his wife's death was something he didn't wish to discuss. She tucked the information away for future consideration and steered the conversation in another direction that piqued her interest. "You said your husband fought for the North."

"It's a very sore spot with many people, but Colton did what he believed was right." Auralie's voice rang with pride for her husband.

"I can imagine. Dale has told me a little about his time during the war." A tiny light of understanding emerged in Charity's mind. She suddenly felt very privileged that Dale had shared with her as much as he had. "When I first met your brother, it was to ask him about a former slave I'm seeking. He is my friend's son. His name is Wylie, and he belonged to Covington Plantation from the time he was thirteen, but Dale didn't remember him."

"Wylie?" Auralie put one finger to her chin. "When I was a young girl, I used to sneak down to the slave quarters to visit with some of the children. I taught a few of them to read until my father found out. But I don't remember anyone named Wylie. I'm sorry."

Admiration for her new friend filled Charity. "It must have taken a great deal of courage to teach slave children to read when you were only a child yourself."

"My father called me rebellious, not courageous." A rueful smile wobbled across Auralie's face. "Maybe Barnabas knows him. Barnabas was a slave before Colton bought him and freed him. He lives by us and works with Colton. I'll ask him when we get home."

"Meanwhile I'll keep looking." Charity shifted her package of paper to her other hand. "I'm also searching for information about my father. He was an officer in the Union army, but he never came home from the war."

Sympathy etched lines across Auralie's brow. "I'm so sorry."

Charity acknowledged the woman's compassion with a slight nod. "I'm hoping to find some records that might tell me what became of him after he was wounded and captured."

Auralie pointed down the street. "Here comes Colton. He might be able to give you some information."

A wagon driven by a handsome man wearing a black coat pulled up in front of the general store.

"Papa! We got peppermint sticks!" Rose and Timothy clambered into their father's arms the moment he alighted from the wagon. He ruffled Timothy's hair and caressed his daughter's cheek.

Auralie reached for her husband's arm. "Colton, this is Miss Charity Galbraith. She and I have become friends."

Colton pulled his hat off. "Miss Charity. I've been hearing about you. It's nice to meet you."

"Likewise, Mr. Danfield."

His wife slipped her arm through his. "Colton, Charity's father was an officer with the Union army, and she is looking for information about him. I wondered if you could help her."

"If I can." Colton looked from Auralie to Charity. "What is it you're trying to find?"

Charity's heart accelerated with hopeful anticipation. "My father was Major Charles Hampton Galbraith, and he served under Major General Oliver Howard with the Fourth Army Corps. The last my mother and I heard was that he'd been wounded and taken prisoner at a place called Pickett's Mill."

A flicker of recognition lit Colton's eyes. "I started out

with General George Thomas and the Army of the Cumberland, but I was briefly with the Fourth Army Corps in May of 1864. I was returned to Tennessee just before the battle at Pickett's Mill."

Charity's heart soared, and her breath quickened. "So you might have known my father?" A tremble ran through her.

"Major Galbraith?" Colton frowned in concentration. "I seem to remember a Galbraith. Tall, dark hair with gray streaks in it, thick mustache, soft spoken."

Tears of joy and anguish intertwined and gave Charity's heart a release of its long pent-up ache. She covered a tiny sob with her fingers. "Yes, that sounds like my father. He always said people would listen more closely if one spoke quietly."

Auralie touched Charity's arm.

A thread of caution laced Colton's tone. "I didn't really know him. I only remember him briefly. The battles at New Hope Church and Pickett's Mill occurred after I was sent back to the Army of the Cumberland, so I'm afraid I can't tell you what happened after that."

While a drop of disappointment trickled through her, the joy of speaking with someone who remembered her father—even for a short time—sent encouragement coursing through her veins.

"Perhaps you can tell me where I might find the prisoner of war records."

Colton pressed his lips together. "Hmm. I know the records for the Federal Army are kept in Washington, but the Confederate records aren't there. They might be in Milledgeville, but I'm not sure. I wish I could be of more help."

"Just speaking with someone who knew Father means so

much to me." Tears burned the back of her throat. "Thank you for that."

Auralie reached over and squeezed Charity's hand. "I'm so glad we met, and I wish we could stay and chat, but we really must be going."

Charity returned the squeeze. "Will I see you tomorrow at church?"

"We'll be there." Colton picked up his wife's basket and deposited it behind the wagon seat, and then swung the youngsters into the back. He held his wife's hand while she climbed aboard then turned to tip his hat to Charity. "It was nice to meet you, Miss Galbraith. Good day to you."

Charity hugged the package of paper tightly against her and waved as the Danfield family wagon rolled down the street. Emotions tumbled within her. Dale's sister was a dear person, her children adorable, and her husband a man of character. His description of her father sang in her ears. But the thing that tugged for her attention was learning that Dale had been married. Why did it bother her that he hadn't told her?

Dale locked the office door and descended the stairs. He always welcomed the end of a long work week, but never more so than this one. Tate Ridley had done his best to antagonize him for the past three days—ever since Simon left for the logging camp. Even though Dale had a half day of making deliveries for the general store ahead of him, he looked forward to a day and a half without having to deal with Ridley.

Some additional paperwork had kept him a few extra minutes, and Clyde was probably wondering where he was. He hurried to the bottom of the steps, but before he went ten feet, a shiny glint caught his eye. He stopped and bent to take a closer look.

A silver chain lay in the dirt. Dale picked it up and examined it. He couldn't remember if Simon wore a silver watch chain. This one had an oval fob with an oak leaf carved into it. Made sense, he supposed, that a man who worked in the timber business would have a watch fob with an oak leaf, but Dale simply hadn't noticed it before. It had to be Simon's. He'd never seen anyone else around the lumberyard with something like that. Strange, he hadn't noticed it lying on the ground before now, but he'd been busy the past couple of days, and had much on his mind.

He was already late getting to the general store, so rather than climb the stairs and lock the chain in the desk, Dale slipped it into his pocket. Simon wouldn't be back until next week anyway. Dale figured to tuck the chain into the desk drawer first thing Monday morning.

He hastened across the bridge and decided to cut through the trees and the alley that ran between the bank and the post office to save time. Halfway down the alley, an unwelcomed voice hailed him.

"Covington."

Dale groaned. Couldn't he just pretend he didn't hear and keep going? He heaved a sigh and turned. "What is it, Tate?"

Ridley came sauntering up to him. Had the man been following him?

"I hear tell you and that Yankee reporter been goin' to church together." He grinned at his companion, the same man who had harassed Charity a week and a half earlier. "Mighty holier-than-thou if you ask me."

"Is there a point to this, Ridley? I need to get to the mercantile."

Ridley lifted his shoulders and held out his hands. "Just appears like she's settlin' in to stay. Thought by now you'd be tryin' to get shed of her. 'Course maybe you got yourself other reasons for keepin' her close." Ridley and his friend guffawed.

Dale stiffened and curled his fingers into fists. "You better watch your mouth, Ridley." Acid crawled up Dale's throat at Ridley's insinuations.

"I ain't sayin' nothin' that ain't so." Ridley waggled his eyebrows. "She ain't too bad to look at. The two of you got ya a cozy arrangement goin' on?"

Dale growled from the pit of his stomach and connected his fist with Ridley's jaw. The man sprawled in the dirt holding his hand to his mouth.

Dale spread his feet and braced himself, waiting for Ridley to get up.

Ridley pulled himself to his feet and spit blood. "C'mon. You think you're better'n me?"

Arms gripped Dale from behind and Ridley rammed his fist into Dale's middle. A moment later the two men were throwing punches high and low. Dale bellowed with rage, putting every ounce of strength he had into a right hook.

Ridley ducked and Dale fell off balance. Ridley leaped onto Dale and began driving punches into Dale's face. Dale rolled and shoved Ridley into the dirt, the two of them wrestling for control.

A steel-like grip dug fingers into Dale's shoulder and pulled him off Ridley, depositing him on his backside up against the building. Miles Flint then yanked Ridley up by his shirt.

"What's going on here?" The sheriff's gruff demand rang through the alley.

Dale rubbed his jaw and stood gingerly, holding his ribs. "He just needs to learn some manners."

"That ain't so, sheriff," Ridley yelled, pointing at Dale. "He stole my watch chain. Look in his pocket."

"What?" Dale stared at Ridley, momentarily speechless.

He shook his head, trying to dislodge the cobwebs. Surely he didn't hear correctly.

Miles tossed Dale a look over his shoulder. "You have his watch chain in your pocket?"

Dale tried to straighten, but the pain in his ribs grabbed him. "How did he know I had that watch chain in my pocket?"

Miles turned halfway around and nailed Dale with a hard stare. "You mean you *do* have his watch chain?"

"Yes, but—I mean, no. I didn't know it was—I found it." Dale groped to put the pieces together in his mind.

Miles checked Dale's pockets and extracted the silver chain.

"See there, I told you, sheriff." Ridley fairly crowed. "He stole my watch chain, and I was just tryin' to get it back."

Dale pointed at Ridley. "Miles, surely you don't believe I'd steal a watch chain or anything else. I found it lying in the dirt over at the sawmill. I thought it was Simon's. I was going to lock it up in the office, but I was already late getting to the mercantile."

Miles looked from Dale to Ridley and back to Dale. He slipped the chain into his vest pocket and took hold of Dale's arm. "Come on, Dale."

"What? Miles, you know me better than that."

"Dale, I got no choice. Tate, here, says you stole his watch chain. The watch chain is in your pocket. Until I can untangle this mess, I'm going to have to lock you up."

As Dale walked up the alley toward the jail with Miles, Ridley's evil laugh followed him.

Chapter 14

"Arrested!"

Charity blurted the word as if it tasted bad on her tongue. Surely Hannah must be mistaken. The distress in her landlady's voice said otherwise.

"Yes." Hannah stood in the doorway of Charity's room, wringing the corner of her apron between her fingers. "Dale and Tate got into a fight, and Tate said Dale stole his watch. Miles arrested Dale."

Charity grabbed her shawl and bonnet. "This is preposterous. Dale would never do such a thing." She yanked her bonnet on and tossed the shawl around her shoulders.

Hannah followed her down the stairs, and Charity paused by the front door. "I'll be back as soon as I can. Try not to worry."

Charity marched out the door and lengthened her strides once past the gate. She placed one hand on her head to keep her bonnet from blowing off in her haste. Minutes later, she stepped in the door of the sheriff's office.

"Mr. Flint, what is the meaning of this? Have you lost your mind? How could you possibly believe Dale is guilty of stealing a watch? This is the most ridiculous, absurd, outrageous—"

The sheriff rose from his desk and held up his hand. "Whoa." He pulled an extra chair out from behind a cabinet and positioned it opposite his. "Have a seat."

Charity plunked both fists on her hips. "I don't feel like sitting. I demand you release Dale at once."

Flint heaved a loud sigh. " 'Fraid I can't do that just yet." He pointed to the chair. "Have a seat."

She narrowed her eyes at the man. "I don't want to sit."

Flint placed his hands on the desk and leaned forward. "I didn't ask you if you *wanted* to sit. Have a seat."

Steaming, Charity gathered her skirts and plopped into the chair, her arms folded across her chest and one foot tapping on the floor.

Flint sat at his desk and picked up a stubby pencil. "First of all, Dale didn't steal a watch. Tate Ridley said he stole his watch chain. Secondly, if it's any comfort to you, you're not the first person who's come in here in the past hour *demandin'* that I release him. I thought Clyde Sawyer was gonna climb over my desk and grab my keys, and I almost had to arrest his wife! The preacher clucked his tongue at me. The Ferguson ladies were pert near in tears, and Miss Hannah—" He shook his head. "I won't be surprised if she throws me out of the boardinghouse on my ear. I might have to sleep in the jail tonight, myself!"

Charity harrumphed. "Shouldn't that tell you something? If all those people believe Dale is innocent, how can you possibly keep him in jail?"

Flint leaned back in his chair. "Because the watch chain

was in Dale's pocket." He tossed the pencil on the desk. "I can let you see him as soon as Doc Greenway is finished—"

Charity leaped from her chair. "Doctor? What's the matter with Dale?"

The old, gray-haired doctor Charity remembered interviewing a couple of weeks ago stepped through the door that led to the cells. "Afternoon, Miss Galbraith." He set his shabby black bag on the chair Charity had vacated. "I bandaged him up, Miles. He has a couple of cracked ribs, and some cuts and bruises. I've seen worse."

Charity's breath seemed to escape involuntarily. "But how—"

"He and Tate were goin' at it in the alley when I come up on them," Flint explained. "Doc, how much do I owe you?"

Doctor Greenway waved his hand. "Not a thing. Dale's a fine man. If you want my opinion, Miles Flint, I think you're a lunatic for keeping him in jail." He gave a snort and a sharp nod of his head to punctuate his statement, snatched his bag, and stomped out the door.

Flint rolled his eyes and sighed. "I suppose you'll be wantin' to see him now?"

Charity didn't answer but marched toward the inner door, tossing a look over her shoulder at the sheriff to make sure he followed.

Dale lay on a narrow cot in the small cell. Charity gasped when she caught a glimpse of his swollen eye, bruised face, and cut lip. Her stomach turned over at the sight of the bandages swathed around his ribs. Her heart thudded in her chest like a sledgehammer.

"Dale, I came as soon as I heard. Oh my soul, are you all right?" She couldn't keep her voice steady.

Dale released a muffled groan as he sat up. "I'm all right. Just a little sore." His cut lip slightly distorted his speech.

A basin of water and a cloth sat on the floor beside the cot. Charity turned to Flint. "Can you let me in there?"

The sheriff smirked and grasped one iron bar of the door. It swung open without benefit of Flint's key. "Take as long as you want." He turned back toward his office. "I'll just leave this here door open for propriety's sake."

Charity slipped into the cell, a shudder rattling through her middle. She hesitated. Despite the open door, it wasn't seemly to sit beside Dale on the cot. The sheriff read her mind.

"Thought you might want this chair." He carried the chair Charity had used in the outer office through the cell door and placed it opposite the cot.

Dale tilted his head, a painful grimace on his face. "Thanks, Miles."

Charity sat and scooted the chair a bit closer to him. "Dale, I don't understand. How in the world did this happen?"

"I'm still trying to figure that out myself." He shifted position and winced. "I already told Miles my side of the story."

"Would you mind telling me?" She took the cloth, dipped it in the basin of water, and gently placed it against Dale's swollen eye. "You don't have to if you don't want to, but I'd like to hear it from you. I promise I won't put it in my articles."

Dale tried to chuckle but instead held his hand to his ribs. "Ooh." He took a few shallow breaths. "I was finished for the day at the sawmill. I'd run a little late because there was some paperwork I needed to finish. I locked the office door and went down the steps. Not far from the stairs I saw something glinting in the sunlight. I picked it up. It was a watch chain and fob."

She blotted his cut lip and rinsed the cloth again while Dale went on.

"I don't remember seeing it before, but I figured it must belong to Simon. I thought it was strange, though, because Simon left for the logging camp a couple of days ago. If he dropped it, I should have seen it lying there before today. Guess I just had too much on my mind and didn't notice it."

"How did Tate come to accuse you of stealing it?" She tenderly laid the cool rag on his face again.

"That's another thing I can't figure out." He gave an almost imperceptible shake of his head. "Because I was late, I cut through a couple of yards and alleys to save time. It's not the way I normally go, but Tate came up behind me, almost like he was following me. That man who accosted you the other day was with him. Tate started saying some rude things. I told him to watch his mouth, but he kept on, making some very crass and insulting remarks, so I punched him in the mouth and knocked him down. Next thing I know, that other fellow grabbed me from behind, and Tate and I were fighting. When Miles showed up, Tate started yelling about me stealing his watch chain."

Charity pulled the cloth back. "He didn't mention the chain when he first approached you?"

"No."

"Did you tell the sheriff about this?"

Miles Flint's voice reached her from the front room. "Every word. I got it wrote down."

Charity sat back in her chair. "This doesn't make sense."

"It doesn't make sense to me, either, but Miles says he has to keep me here until he can untangle the facts."

She rose and set the basin down. "You need to rest. I'll be back later." She turned her head toward the door and raised her voice a tad. "If the sheriff will let me."

"I'll let you," Flint called out. "In fact, I might need you to bring us both something to eat from Maybelle's if Miss Hannah refuses to feed me."

She paused at the cell door and then returned to the chair. She leaned forward and lowered her voice to nearly a whisper. "Dale, may I ask you something?"

"Anything."

"Why didn't you tell me you were married?"

Dale lay on the cot with one hand tucked behind his head. Why didn't he tell Charity about Gwendolyn? The only reason that kept prodding him was he'd also have to tell her—

"Dale, you want another cup of coffee?"

Dale groaned. Two nights of sleeping on the lumpy cot and drinking Miles's coffee hadn't improved his mood. He called back to Miles. "Is it Maybelle's coffee or yours?"

"You gettin' picky?"

Dale leaned against the wall of his cell. "I just don't like coffee that I have to chew."

The front door of the office opened. The legs of Miles's chair scraped against the floor. "Mornin', Simon. Guess I know why you're here."

Dale pulled himself up from the cot and came out of the cell that Miles hadn't bothered to lock. He'd wondered for the past two days how he was going to tell Simon about this.

Simon pulled his hat off and scratched his head. "When I got to the mill this morning and there wasn't anyone there, I knew something was wrong. Ran into Ned Caldwell, and he told me you and Tate got in a fight and you got arrested." He peered closer at Dale's face. "I sure hope you made him look worse."

Dale gave him a tiny smirk. "I threw the first punch."

Simon grinned. "Good for you." He looked at Miles.

"You must not consider him too desperate a criminal if you're leaving his cell unlocked."

Miles poured coffee into a tin mug and pushed it across the desk toward Simon. "Sit down. I'll tell you all about it."

Miles pulled the watch chain out of the drawer and laid it on the desk. "You ever seen this before?"

Simon took at look at the chain and fob. "No."

Dale poured himself a half cup of coffee and grimaced at the first sip. "I found it in the dirt. I thought it was yours."

Simon shook his head. "Not mine. Miles, this is the worst coffee I ever tasted."

Dale watched Simon's face as he related his side of the story. Other than a raised eyebrow or two, his boss didn't seem at all surprised.

Simon set his coffee mug on the desk and turned to the sheriff. "I guess it's time I tell you what I saw three Friday nights ago."

Dale sat on the edge of the desk while Simon told Miles about hearing a commotion by the Athens road the night of the lynching. "I recognized Tate's voice."

Miles tilted backward in his chair. "What were you doing out there at that time of night?"

"I was going home, and my horse threw a shoe. Pulled up lame. I couldn't ride him, and I knew I'd never make it to town before dark walking, so I made camp."

Dale watched Miles roll the story over in his mind.

"Hmm. I believe you, but that doesn't prove Dale's innocent."

"How long you going to keep my foreman in jail?"

Dale looked at the sheriff, very interested to know the answer to that question.

"Unless I can find proof that Dale didn't steal the chain, I'm gonna have to keep him here till the circuit judge comes around again." Miles sent Dale an apologetic look. "That won't be for another two weeks."

"Two weeks!" Dale slid off the corner of the desk and thrust his arms out at his sides, immediately regretting the action. He rubbed his sore ribs.

Simon stood and nodded at Dale. "Appears like you need to rest up anyway." He picked up his hat. "Can I bring you anything?"

Dale snorted. "Some decent coffee."

Dale sat across the desk from Miles, concentrating on the chess board and munching on the sugar cookies Charity had brought earlier. "I hope you don't have plans for this queen." He slid his bishop diagonally and captured the sheriff's key piece.

Miles blew out through pursed lips. "Can't you let me win just one game?"

Dale grinned. "I will if you let me out of here."

"I might just lock that cell and—"

The office door creaked open, and a thin black woman tapped on the doorframe. "All right iffen I come in?"

Miles eyed her. "Come on in. What do you need?"

Her hair was covered by a kerchief, and her blue dress was faded and patched, but clean. "I hear'd about two men gittin' in a fight, and one of 'em stole'd a silver watch chain."

Miles frowned and narrowed his eyes at her. "Where'd you hear that?"

She lowered her eyes and shrugged. "Talk gits around, even out in Crow Town. Come to see fo' myself."

Miles pointed at her. "Aren't you the wife of the man…"

"Yes, suh." Her voice broke, but she lifted her chin slightly. "I be Annie Jarrell. My man, Henry, be the one that them no account drunkards lynched."

Dale stood and offered Mrs. Jarrell his chair, but she shook her head.

The sheriff's tone softened. "What is it you're askin', Miz Jarrell?"

She drew in a deep breath, as if what she was about to say was going to cost her dearly. "The night they came and dragged my Henry away, I followed, so's I can see where they take him. But I got lost. I listen hard, but all I hear'd was wind howlin' like a mournful thing. A while later I see a cross burnin', and I know…I know what they done to my Henry." She wiped tears away with her fists.

"When our men went and cut Henry down from that tree, and they's gittin' him ready for buryin', I looked through his pockets. His daddy's watch chain was missin'. Henry's daddy was Eli Jarrell. Eli's massah set him free befo' the war, and the massah give Eli his old watch chain. Eli, he never had no watch to hang from it, but he be mighty proud o' that chain. When Eli died, Henry took the chain, and he carry wid him all th' time, 'cause it be the onliest thing he have to remind him o' his daddy."

Grief strained her voice. "When they hang my Henry, whoever done it stole his daddy's watch chain." The set of her jaw defined her anger. "Mm-hmm. Then I hear'd tell 'bout a watch chain turnin' up here."

Dale and Miles exchanged looks, and Miles rubbed his chin. "Miz Jarrell, can you describe the watch chain for me?"

" 'Course I can. It be the color of moonlight, and it be as long as from the tip o' my pointer finger to my elbow. The piece a-danglin' from one end have a oak leaf on it, and there be a li'l nick near the tip o' the leaf. The seventh link in the chain is crooked where it broke one time and Henry do the best he can to fix it."

Miles reached in the desk drawer and pulled out the

chain. Mrs. Jarrell covered her mouth as she gave a little joyful cry. Miles stretched it out on the desk and counted the links. The seventh link had a slightly odd shape and the oak leaf fob had a tiny nick at the tip.

Dale reached over and scooped up the chain, picked up Mrs. Jarrell's hand, and laid the chain in her palm. She raised tear-filled eyes to him. "Thank ya kindly, suh."

Miles walked her to the door. "Be careful goin' home, Miz Jarrell."

Dale stared at the door after Miles closed it. "Is that enough proof?"

Miles crossed to the desk. "That you're innocent?"

Dale turned and locked eyes with the sheriff. "That Tate is guilty."

Chapter 15

Charity sipped her coffee. "Hannah, how well do you know Dale?"

Her landlady stirred a few drops of cream into her cup. "I know him better now than I did before the war."

"Did you know he was married?"

Hannah raised her cup to her lips and looked at Charity over the rim. "Yes."

Charity shoved aside her mild annoyance that nobody had bothered to mention Dale's marriage. Why should they? Dale's personal life was none of her business, and Hannah wasn't one to gossip. However, the older woman must have detected Charity's unsettled chafing because she lowered her cup and reached across the kitchen table to cover Charity's hand.

"It wasn't my place to say anything." Hannah's gentle tone stroked Charity's heart. "He was married just before the war. There was a notice in the *Sentinel*. The wedding didn't take place here in town. They were a very wealthy family and had no use for our little church." No cynicism laced her voice. "The town folk simply didn't know a great deal about his wife other than her name—Gwendolyn. She very rarely came into town and didn't have contact with the 'common people,' if you know what I mean. I think her family was from the Athens area.

"I remember seeing Dale from time to time during the war, but like most, he was gone for long periods. You remember I told you that scavengers looted and burned the manor house at Covington Plantation. Nobody here in town knows for sure what happened, but I think Gwendolyn died around that time. Dale doesn't talk about it."

Charity's stomach turned over, imagining the grief Dale experienced. No wonder he was withdrawn. A new ache— a different ache—kindled within her. But this pain wasn't born of anger toward the Rebels. It was saturated with sympathy for one Rebel—one who had quietly, softly, become very dear to her. When she'd asked him a few days ago why he'd never told her about his marriage, she'd thought it a reasonable question until she saw the haunted look in his eyes. Now the memory of it struck her, and she regretted having put that expression of pain on his face.

Hannah didn't appear to notice Charity's discomfiture as she traced the rim of her coffee cup with her finger. "When Dale came home, he'd been wounded. The first time I saw him at the end of the war, he was like a broken thing—a mere shadow of the man he'd been. Within months, carpetbaggers came through the area and began buying up land cheap. He lost everything."

The front door opened, and Charity recognized Miles Flint's voice.

"Miss Hannah?"

Hannah pressed her lips together and sent a look of exasperation to Charity. "That man! I'm still perturbed at him for putting Dale in jail." She called out, "In the kitchen."

Miles, hat in hand, poked his head through the kitchen door. "Got a man here who could use a cup of coffee. He doesn't like mine." Dale's face came into view behind Miles.

Charity's heart fluttered as Dale's gaze locked onto hers. Something unspoken bridged the space between them, and she rose from her chair. If he was angry that she'd asked about his wife, it didn't show. He looked straight at her, as if there were no one else in the room. She couldn't have torn her gaze away if she wanted to—and she didn't want to.

Dale's pulse accelerated when Charity's gaze connected with his. His concern for her safety defied definition. He'd been aware for a couple of weeks that he cared about her, but with the confirmation of Tate's involvement with the lynching, coupled with the remarks he'd made about "that Yankee woman," sweet relief swept over his heart at seeing her at Miss Hannah's kitchen table.

Her lips parted. Did she want to say something? Apparently deciding this wasn't the time or place, she pressed her lips together into the tiniest of smiles.

Miss Hannah plunked her hands on her hips and glowered at Miles. "So you finally found your common sense and let him out." She crossed the cupboard and pulled out two coffee mugs.

"Miss Hannah, have you seen Tate Ridley?"

Hannah paused in midmotion pouring coffee into the mugs. "Why, no. He wasn't at breakfast, but I just assumed he left early."

Miles and Dale exchanged a look. "We already checked at the mill. He's not there, and Simon hasn't seen him either."

Miles scowled and pursed his lips. "Miss Hannah, could I trouble you to go up and check Tate's room?"

"Of course, but what am I looking for?"

"I'll come with you." He followed Hannah from the room.

Charity stepped over to the stove and finished pouring the coffee. She handed a brimming cup to Dale. "Peace offering?"

Dale accepted the steaming, fragrant brew. "For what?"

Charity's hands fidgeted at her waist. "Dale, I'm sorry. Asking about your wife was none of my business. I should have known better, and I didn't mean to offend you."

He gave a slight shrug. "You didn't. I should have told you sooner." He lifted the mug close to his lips and inhaled the bracing aroma. "Not talking about it won't change what happened."

She returned to the table and reclaimed her seat. "At least you can go to the cemetery and put flowers on the graves of your parents and your wife. That must be some comfort to you."

A chill raced through him, and an involuntary tremble shook the coffee in his cup so that it nearly sloshed over the rim.

Charity's gentle words carried a thread of sorrow. "I wish I knew where my father was buried. I've assumed for a long time that he's dead, but if I could just visit his grave and lay some flowers there, it would be like telling him good-bye."

He found his voice, but couldn't push much more than a mumble past his lips. "My...family—" He swallowed the lump of bitterness in his throat. "They aren't buried in the cemetery. They're buried at Covington Plantation, or at least what used to be Covington Plantation, on land I no longer own."

He couldn't look at her because he was afraid the sympathy he'd surely see in her eyes would be his undoing. Instead, he studied the black liquid in his cup and took a deep breath, as if coaxing the aroma to his nostrils.

Hannah bustled into the kitchen followed by Miles. Dale looked up at the sheriff. A frown troubled the man's brow.

"It's as I feared. All Tate's things are gone. He probably cleared out during the night."

The events of the past hour tumbled through Dale's mind, and he shot a pointed look at Miles. "Are you thinking what I'm thinking?"

"Mrs. Jarrell?"

"You think she's safe?"

Miles grabbed his hat. "Only one way to find out."

Dale set his cup down. "Do you want me to come with you?"

Miles hesitated a moment. "No." His gaze slid briefly to Charity. "It's probably best that you stay in town." He strode out the door.

Charity and Hannah exchanged a glance. "Who is Mrs. Jarrell?"

Dale held out his coffee cup. "If I can have more of that magnificent coffee, I'll tell you about it."

By the time he finished telling Charity and Hannah about the woman and her story of the watch chain, their coffee was cold and there were tears in Charity's eyes.

"What an incredibly brave woman."

Dale nodded, but he looked with new eyes into Charity's heart and saw a woman of similar courage. She'd undertaken a task many men would avoid and had not flinched when her mission took her into dangerous territory. And the feeling he had for her went far beyond admiration.

* * *

Charity heaved a sigh of relief at supper when Miles told her he'd caught up with Mrs. Jarrell and escorted her the rest of the way to Crow Town. Speculation skittered around the table over Tate Ridley's disappearance.

Arch Wheeler smirked. "I knew he was trouble the first time I laid eyes on him." His tone suggested everyone present should compliment him on his discernment. Instead, the sheriff cautioned all the boarders to rein in their imaginations and not start any rumors.

The Ferguson ladies helped with dessert and coffee while Charity carried dishes into the kitchen for Hannah. The landlady scraped thin peels of lye soap into the dishpan and added steaming water from the stove. Suds began to form and suddenly Hannah gasped.

"Oh, Charity! I just thought of something. Oh, why didn't I think of this earlier? I'm getting to be so cloudy-headed. That's what happens when a body starts getting old. I'm so sorry, dear."

Had it not been for the distress on Hannah's face, Charity might have laughed. "What are you sorry for?"

Hannah grabbed a towel and wiped her hands. "The laundress at the hotel. Her name is Ivy. You should talk to her."

Charity stared at her, wondering if the dear soul had been working too hard. "The laundress?"

Hannah caught Charity's hands. "She is a former slave, and she's been in these parts a long time. I know it's an awfully slim chance, but maybe she knows something about the man you're looking for."

A tiny flame of hope kindled in her heart, and Charity cautioned herself not to fan it into a bonfire, at least not yet.

She excused herself and scurried upstairs to work on her articles, but unable to concentrate, she sat by the small window and looked out at the winking stars. "Heavenly Father, is this woman, Ivy, the one who will lead me to Wylie?" The heavens didn't reply, but the hope in her heart wasn't quenched. She snuffed out the lamp and tried to close her eyes. The images that formed were of Essie embracing her son.

After fighting with the bedcovers most of the night, Charity turned down sausage and eggs for breakfast. Her stomach couldn't handle much more than a piece of bread and cup of coffee. She chided herself again with the warning that this woman might turn out to be one more dead end.

Charity could barely restrain her feet to a ladylike pace. Each purposeful step carried her closer to the hotel. "Please, Lord, I pray this woman will be able to open the door to finding Wylie."

Instead of entering the hotel lobby where the desk clerk would, no doubt, discourage her from seeking the laundress, she cut down the alley between the hotel and the saloon. Behind the hotel, Charity discovered a half-dozen clotheslines stretched between the building and the broad back fence. Freshly washed sheets flapped from two of the lines. A Negro woman with gray frizzy hair peeking out from beneath a blue kerchief stood at the third line. She pulled a sparkling white sheet from the basket at her feet and began pinning it to the line. While she worked, she hummed a tune around the clothespins stuck in her mouth.

"Excuse me, ma'am."

The woman spun around and grabbed the clothespins from her mouth. She cast a distrustful gaze at Charity.

"Is your name Ivy?"

The woman didn't answer but glanced around warily before directing her eyes back at Charity.

Charity offered her a smile and approached easily. "I don't mean you any harm. Are you Ivy?"

The laundress nodded slowly.

"My name is Charity, and Mrs. Sparrow at the boardinghouse suggested I might come and talk with you. Would you mind?"

Ivy's eyes read like a book. She clearly didn't trust anyone with white skin.

Noise from the saloon next door spilled out every time the door opened, and Charity had to raise her voice. "Please, Miss Ivy?"

A glimmer of confusion, followed by a hint of amusement, flickered across the woman's face, and Charity wondered when was the last time anyone said *please* to her.

"I hope you can help me. I live in Pennsylvania—a long way from here, and I have a friend there. She used to be a slave, and she was at the Talbot Plantation. Her name is Essie."

A brief glint of recognition lit Ivy's eyes, and she nodded slowly. "I 'member Essie."

Joy flooded Charity's heart, and she clasped her hands at her chest. "You do?" She drew closer to Ivy. "Do you happen to remember she had a son?"

Ivy dropped her gaze to the basket of wet laundry and then looked toward the hotel. "I has work I gots to do."

"Of course." Charity tried to keep her excitement in check. "Let me help you."

Ivy's mouth dropped open and her eyes widened. "Oh no, missy. I cain't let you do that."

"Nonsense, I've hung plenty of laundry, and I don't want you to get into trouble." She took a wet sheet from the basket and shook it out. "Essie is my dear friend, and she hasn't seen her son for more than eleven years." She pinned the sheet securely to the line. "By any chance do you remember her son? His name—"

"His name was Wylie."

Charity almost dropped the clothespins in her hand. "Yes! Yes, you remember him?"

Ivy's voice took on a pensive tone and her eyes, a faraway look. "I 'member when Essie first come to Talbot. She weren't but twelve years old, and the massah put her in the kitchen."

Laughter and bawdy music from the saloon made it difficult to hear Ivy, as soft-spoken as she was. Charity moved closer to her and hung on her every word.

"Essie work in the kitchen, and when she get older, dey teach her to sew. When she was…maybe eighteen or nineteen, one o' the field hands catch her eye. His name be Abe, and he and Essie, dey fall in love right off." Ivy moved to the next clothesline and Charity moved with her, unwilling to miss a single word.

"Essie and Abe, dey jump de broom, but the massah, he don't know. Dey keep the secret. The other slaves, dey know, but nobody tell the massah. Essie and Abe, dey be together when dey can, but the massah say he be the one who decide which slave he breed.

"Essie come up in the family way. She try to hide it, but dey ain't no hidin' sumpin' like dat fo' long. Massah, he get real angry, and he whip Essie, even though her time gettin' close. But he don' whip Abe, no. He sell Abe so dey cain't be together no mo'."

Tears burned Charity's eyes, and she gripped the clothespins so tightly they dug into her flesh.

Ivy pinned another sheet up before continuing. "Essie's baby come, and it be a li'l boy chile. I 'member she name him Wylie. Some o' us ask why she don't name him Abe after his daddy, and she say she 'fraid if she name him

Abe, massah will sell him, too. Massah let Essie keep her boy till he be thirteen year, and old 'nough to work in da field." She shook her head. "Mmm-mm."

The tears Charity tried to blink back escaped down her cheeks.

Ivy's voice tightened. "Massah send dat boy to a slave auction. Essie—her heart near break, even mo' than when massah sell Abe. I thought she gonna grieve herself nigh unto death. She hear'd later Wylie sold to Covington Plantation."

Charity wiped the tears from her face and sniffed. Poor Essie. What cruel heartache she'd suffered.

"Do you know where Wylie is now?"

Ivy dipped her chin and shook her head. "He meybe be sold again, or meybe he run off when the war started. Some went North. Some massahs send their slaves to fight in the war, so lots of dem probably in da grave by now. Dere's some colored folk live out by Athens road, a place called Crow Town." She halted and turned abruptly to face Charity. "But you don' go out dere, missy. No, Crow Town ain't no place fo' the likes o' you." Ivy reached out bony fingers and grasped Charity's hand. "You promise ole Ivy, you don' go out dere."

A chill slithered through Charity's middle, but it wasn't from Ivy's cold hands.

Chapter 16

Charity couldn't resist the urge to enfold Ivy in a hug. The woman widened her eyes in astonishment as Charity released her.

"Thank you so much, Ivy. You'll never know how much this means to me."

Ivy lowered her eyes. "I hope Essie get to see her boy again."

A prick of wonderment held Charity in place for an extra moment. Had Ivy suffered a similar loss? Charity didn't want to pry. Instead, she squeezed Ivy's hand.

"I promise you, Ivy, I'm going to do everything I can to see that happen."

When Ivy looked up at her, a small light sparked to life in the woman's eyes. "I be prayin' the good Lawd go wid you."

Charity hurried down the alley between the hotel and the saloon, her feet pounding out the rhythm of the tinny piano music. She couldn't wait until the workday was over to tell Dale her news.

She snatched both corners of her shawl as she set her course for the sawmill. Dale was certain to be as excited as—

Charity skidded to a halt. The same two men who had harassed her before stood near the entrance of the alley, their arms folded across their chests. She drew in a shaky breath and proceeded forward with sure strides.

The man on the right spoke first. "We want to talk to you, lady."

"Well, I don't have time to talk to you, right now, so if you'll excuse me, please."

The man on the left moved to block her path. "You don't need to talk. All you gotta do is listen."

Her heart galloped and moisture popped out on her brow despite the cool air. "Don't you two have anything better to do than bully women?"

The first man scowled at her. "You didn't listen too good the first time we talked, so we're gonna make real sure you hear us this time." He pulled out a pocket knife and toyed with it. "You been doin' lots of talkin' all over town, and we don't like it. You think you're so high and mighty, comin' down here and writin' for your fancy Yankee magazine, stirrin' up the darkies with your questions." He reached out and grabbed the corner of her shawl.

Charity's breath caught and her throat strangled, as if the man gripped her by the neck. The sun glinted off the blade as he slit a six inch gash in her shawl. "If we don't got your attention, Miss Galbraith, we got other ways to do it. So you best listen good, 'cause this here is the last warnin' you're gonna get. We don't like your kind around here. Whatever business you had in Georgia is finished.

It's time for you go home." He held up his knife, turning it first one way and then twisting it around.

The second man took a step closer to her, and the stench of liquor permeated him. A wave of nausea threatened to turn her stomach inside out, but her anger vanquished her fear. She yanked her shawl from the first man's hand and pushed with all her might against his chest. He stumbled backward, whether from the force of her shove or the effect of the drink, it didn't matter.

She barged past both the men and turned to face them once she reached the boardwalk. "Intimidation only makes me more determined than ever."

She spun on her heel and marched across the street where she would be closer to the sheriff's office if needed.

Her insides trembled with each footfall, but she breathed a prayer of thanks for God's protection and kept walking toward the sawmill. She wanted to cast a glance over her shoulder to see if the pair followed, but she refused to allow them to think they'd succeeded. After weeks of searching for someone who could tell her something, anything, about Wylie, she wouldn't let two drunken ruffians steal her joy. She could inform Miles Flint later about the confrontation.

She reached the bridge that crossed to the sawmill and paused, sending her glance scanning the lumberyard in search of Dale. The rhythmic clackety-clacking of the mill kept time with her pulse. Two men loaded lumber onto a wagon and two more worked at cutting what appeared to be fence posts, but none of them were Dale. She shaded her eyes and squinted across to the far side of the yard.

"Charity!"

She turned and saw Dale descending the stairs at the side of the mill. She tucked the damaged corner of her shawl into the thick folds and hurried toward him, but he raised his hand, indicating for her to wait. But she couldn't wait. Her excitement spilled over with giddy enthusiasm.

"I was going to ask if something was wrong, but you look too happy for that," Dale shouted over the racket of the machinery. He nudged her back the way she came. "Let's go across the bridge and talk where it's quieter."

He placed his hand on her back and gently guided her toward a cluster of pines near the edge of Juniper Creek. The thick foliage muted the noise from the sawmill.

"Charity, I don't think it's safe for you to be out alone at this end of town. Miles hasn't found Tate yet, so I'd feel much better if you'd stay closer to the middle of town where there are more people."

She bit her lip. Telling him that the same two men who'd accosted her before had confronted her again would only cause him undue concern. Sticking closer to town wouldn't guarantee safety. The hotel was right in the middle of town. Granted, they'd cornered her in the alley where no one could see them, but calling their bluff rendered their threats hollow.

Dale cupped both her forearms, and his eyes bore deeply into hers. "I wish you wouldn't go out alone, even in the daytime. Not until Miles can track down Tate."

His concern sent warmth spiraling through her, but the urge to share her news with him took priority over his admonition for caution. "Dale, I have something to tell you, and I couldn't wait. I spoke with a woman this morning." She clutched his sleeves. "She remembers Essie and Wylie."

Genuine happiness lit his eyes. "That's wonderful. Who is she? Where did you meet her?" Every bit of the mutual enthusiasm she hoped she'd see and hear in his response was there.

"She works at the hotel. Her name is Ivy, and she's a former slave." She interlaced her fingers to restrain them from flapping with glee. "She was at Talbot Plantation with Essie and remembers when Wylie was born."

Dale took his chin between his thumb and forefinger and his eyebrows dipped in concentration. "Talbot? I served with a Colonel Jerome Talbot in sixty-four. I recall he sometimes kept two or three slaves at some of the encampments. I remember a woman named Ivy. Small, thin. She did laundry and mending for several of the officers."

Charity could barely keep from jumping up and down. "That must be her. She works as a laundress."

Dale pointed to his forehead. "Did she have a little scar right here?"

"Yes, she did." She clasped her hands over her chest. Her heart tripped wildly within her rib cage.

Dale nodded. "Yes, I remember her. She was with the encampment at Ringold Gap and came with us when we moved south to Resaca. Then in May, the colonel sent her and the others to the rear when the fighting took place at New Hope Church and Pickett's Mill. After Kennesaw, we—"

The rest of Dale's words were lost in a fog of shock. Paralysis gripped her, and she forgot how to breathe. A shudder rattled through her, and she began trembling uncontrollably. A rush of heat filled her face and then drained away into the pit of her stomach.

"Charity? What is it? Are you ill? You're as pale a ghost." Dale reached for her, but every nerve ending in her body suddenly found life, and she backed away.

She willed her lips to move. "Pickett's Mill?" Her voice was a hoarse whisper.

"I can't hear you." He moved closer and took her arm. Alarm crept into his voice. "Charity, you look like you're about to faint. Let me help you sit—"

She yanked her arm away. "Pickett's Mill?" The impact of realization that nearly knocked her off her feet moments ago rolled through her again and took root deep in the recesses of her being, growing and heightening until a wave of rage crashed over her. *"Pickett's Mill?"* Her emotions became a runaway locomotive. "You fought at Pickett's Mill?"

Dale's pallor took on the color of a Confederate uniform. His jaw muscles twitched and his chest rose and fell as if he'd just come from the battlefield. "Yes. I was at Pickett's Mill."

She took another step backward, and then another. "You…why didn't you…my father…Pickett's Mill was where he…"

"Charity—"

He reached for her again, and the very motion of his outstretched hand sparked the tinderbox of emotion combusting within her. All the tears and agony she'd bottled up for six years came spewing forth unrestrained.

"How could you? You…you didn't tell me anything… all the times I talked about searching for some scrap of information about my father, and you… All this time, you knew." A storm of rage boiled within her. Every dark, private corner of her heart emptied in a rush of accusation. "You killed him."

Dale's features hardened into a frightful mask of mortal, stunned fury. His fingers curled into tight fists and then stiffened out straight, each appendage taking on the appearance of a weapon. He paled for several long moments. Then the blood surged back into his countenance.

When Dale finally spoke, his voice was a strained hiss. "I was at Pickett's Mill. Many men died there. Some of them from my hands." His chest heaved, and his eyes darkened with aversion. "You don't have any idea…the horror, the nightmares—" He grabbed his head in both hands and a guttural groan emerged from his twisted lips. "The screams of dying men, their pleas for someone to come and end their misery. The blur of wishing I would die and at the same time wanting to live. I had to live. Days of pain and fever wondering if I'd survive to see…"

He bent forward and his knees buckled, as though some unseen force crushed him. "The letter. She sent a letter. I read it over and over. 'Dear Dale, You have a son.' " An excruciating sob wrenched from his throat. "My son…my newborn son. All I wanted was to go home so I could see my son."

He raised his head. His eyes flamed with a pain so brutal, it loomed into a tangible thing between them. Charity held her breath, dreading the words she knew were coming.

"Yankee scavengers didn't just burn my house. They killed my wife and son." The sobs moaned from him like his very lifeblood oozing away. "My son. I never even got to hold him."

The comprehension of the war's evils ravaged the deepest part of Charity's spirit, and her grieving heart splintered and shattered. Each shard bore the name of a loved one who died—some woman's husband, some daughter's father, some father's son. How many arms ached with the longing to hold that one who now lay in a cold, silent grave? A dawning of understanding slowly emerged in her consciousness. Dale's infant son never wore a gray uniform or a blue uniform.

Hot tears coursed down Charity's face, and her feet moved of their own volition. One step, then another. Refuge, was there refuge to hide her from the evil? Faster, *faster*. With no destination or purpose, she simply ran. Through the woods and the hills, she ran. Underbrush reached out long tentacles to snag her skirt and trip her steps, but she pushed forward, not knowing or caring where she went. Was there a place anywhere on this earth where sorrow and pain didn't exist?

Sweat mingled with tears stinging her eyes and leaving salty moisture on her lips. With her heart screaming within her, she kept running. Her lungs nearly burst with the exertion, but as long as the tears flowed, she allowed her feet to carry her.

"God, please hide me under the shadow of Your wings."

Reaching out in front of her, she grasped rocks and saplings, straining to pull herself to the crest of an overlook. Below, the town of Juniper Springs nestled into the valley in idyllic serenity. The tiny houses and miniature structures looked so tranquil and undisturbed from where she stood. Her energy spent, she collapsed onto a bed of fallen leaves and soaked them with her tears, while the presence of God and the music of the wind through the pines whispered peace to her soul.

Dale stumbled through his tasks the rest of the afternoon until Simon finally planted his hands on his hips and glared at him.

"What's got into you, boy? You're acting like you're in love or something."

The idea had occurred to Dale, but hearing someone else say it drove the ramifications home. *Yes, I love her, but she thinks I killed her father.*

Dale mumbled to Simon that he'd see him in the morning and headed across the bridge. The boardinghouse loomed ahead of him. After Charity ran off, he assumed she'd go back to the boardinghouse. What if she was packing to leave? He couldn't let her do that without talking to her again. His raw outburst had nothing to do with her, and there was no way of ever knowing if it was his minié ball that struck down her father.

Somehow giving expression to his deepest, hidden pain was reminiscent of the surgery that repaired his wounds— painful, but cleansing. The festering infection of bitterness released from its prison. Now the healing could begin.

But only if Charity stayed.

Just as Dale reached the boardinghouse, Miles Flint hailed him. The sheriff strode toward him with a grim expression.

"Dale, I just got word that those white-hooded thugs who think it's their duty to rid the South of anyone they consider undesirable are plannin' another get-together tonight." Disgust laced his tone. "I'm gonna ride out to Crow Town and warn everyone to stay inside and bar their doors. You think you could come with me?"

Dale sent a glance in the direction of the boardinghouse. "I have to check on Charity, Miles." He studied the toes of his boots and sucked in a deep breath. "I just want to make sure she came back to the boardinghouse. Once I know she's with Miss Hannah, I'll come with you."

Miles nodded. "I'll be back here in ten minutes with a horse saddled for you."

Dale climbed the front steps of the boardinghouse, and Hannah opened the door to his knock.

"Dale, come in." Tiny lines creased her brow. "Charity isn't here. I was hoping you'd seen her."

Dale's stomach clenched. "How long has she been gone?"

"Since this morning." Hannah picked up the corner of her apron and fidgeted with it. "I told her about the woman who does the laundry at the hotel, and Charity went over there to talk to her, but that was hours ago. I'm beginning to get worried."

Worry wasn't a broad enough term to describe the turmoil in Dale's gut. "If she comes back, you keep her here. I'm going looking for her."

Chapter 17

Dale stuffed extra ammunition into his coat pocket. He filled the reservoir of the lantern with coal oil and patted his shirt pocket to confirm he had a few lucifers tucked there. He picked up his rifle and headed out the door.

Good sense told him the best place to start looking was the spot where he and Charity had spoken earlier that day—the place where she'd accused him of killing her father and where he'd finally relinquished his grip on the pain that had held him captive for six years.

Dale turned the corner and strode toward the boarding-house where Miles Flint waited.

"You ready to go?"

Dale shook his head. "Charity is missing. We…had words earlier, and she ran off into the woods."

"Somethin' upset her today?"

Dale shrugged into his coat. "That's one way of putting it. I'm sorry I can't go with you, but I have to find Charity."

Miles mounted his horse. "Ned Caldwell said he'd go with me. What direction you goin'?"

Dale pointed up the wooded slope. "She ran toward the mountain that way, but there's no telling where she is now."

The sheriff shaded his eyes and looked out across the mountains to the west. "It'll be gettin' dark in another hour. I don't know where those hooligans are goin' either, so you take care." He reined his horse around and headed east toward Crow Town.

Dale leaned the rifle against his shoulder. He returned to the spot where he and Charity had talked earlier and found the place where she'd fled away in tears. As long as he had a bit of daylight, he followed her trail where the underbrush and fallen leaves had been disturbed.

Judging by her direction, she was headed for some wild country. Dale squinted into the glare of the descending sun. Charity had no idea of the danger that lurked on the mountainside, especially after dark. He paused to study her trail. Dismay filled him as he realized she was headed farther away from town. Dale whispered a prayer for her safety and trudged up the steep incline.

Since he didn't know for sure if the "brotherhood" was indeed headed to Crow Town or lurking in the vicinity, he didn't take the chance on calling out Charity's name as he searched.

Shadows gathered like a shroud, cloaking the countryside in veiled mystery. Twilight's brush painted the sky lavender and gold. Casting a wide look across the ridge through the trees revealed no sign of Charity. Dale knew these hills as well as he knew his own name. Charity didn't, and the waning light would disappear all together in another twenty minutes.

He stopped beside a rock outcropping and set the lantern down. He fished a lucifer from his shirt pocket and lit the lantern. It spilled friendly light in a halo around him, but it also marked his location to anyone else roaming about.

Fading light created spooky silhouettes of the bare trees. The promise of frost hung in the air. He looked up into the darkening sky. No clouds hid the stars. He pressed on, lowering the lantern from time to time searching for evidence of Charity's trail.

A rustling noise just ahead stopped him in his tracks. He held the lantern aloft.

"Charity?" His hushed voice echoed like a battle cry through the trees. He flinched and cast a glance around him. "Charity? It's Dale."

"Dale, I'm here."

He swung the lantern to the right and the light danced over her. Her shawl was torn and one of her hands bore some scratches, but she was otherwise all right. He breathed a prayer of thanks. "Charity." He laid his rifle down and set the lantern beside it. "Thank God you're safe." He pulled off his coat and wrapped it around her.

"I'm all right."

He angled his head to peer at her face and tipped her chin up with his fingers. "Are you sure?"

She nodded. "I just ran and ran until I couldn't go any farther, and I lay down in the leaves and cried. I guess I fell asleep."

Dale took hold of her shoulders and gently pulled her to him. "I'm so sorry for the way I blurted all those things at you today. None of that was your fault. I just couldn't seem to stop the words from coming out."

She laid her head on his chest. Having her in his arms sent an ardent shiver through him, and he immediately decided he never wished to let her go.

"I know. While I was up here today, I did a lot of praying." Her voice caught. "Dale, I'm sorry for the horrible things I said to you. Every aspect of the war was so despicable, and it reached far beyond the battlefield." She raised her head and tipped it back to look up at him. The lantern light glimmered off the tear in the corner of her eye. "I had no comprehension of the battle you fought alone, inside you."

He wiped her tear away with his thumb. "We should get back to town."

She tugged at his sleeve. "Can't we stay awhile? It's so peaceful here."

They sat in the leaves side by side and looked out over the valley below. Tiny pinpoints of light speckled here and there showed where the town settled in for the night. Dale laid the rifle beside his leg and set the lantern at their feet.

"Dale, do you mind telling me about your wife?"

Strange. As much as he'd wanted to avoid the subject in weeks past, in the light of what he'd uttered today, sharing the rest no longer seemed repulsive.

"Her name was Gwendolyn. She was…delicate. Shortly after the wedding, my mother died. Then the war broke out, and I went to serve with the state militia. My father took ill, and Gwendolyn couldn't deal with the adversity. She went through periods of melancholia, so the servants told me. She wrote letters begging me to come home. At first I thought it was simply because she'd been overly sheltered all her life.

"I was able to get leave a few times when my unit was close to this area. Each time I went home, she became more and more selfish in her demands until she finally told me if I left her again to 'go back to the war,' that I'd find her gone the next time I came home." He shook his head. "I believe she needed medical supervision, but it was beyond my control at the time."

Charity touched his arm. "Perhaps she was frightened of being alone."

"No." Dale sighed. "I don't think it was that. Many of the house slaves were still here, and she held tea parties and went to Athens regularly. At least that's what I was told, so she wasn't alone. The war hadn't really affected this area too much at that point."

The sequence of events drifted through his head as it had in a thousand nightmares, but this time the pain was dulled. Was it because he'd finally been able to free it from the shackles that kept it bound to his spirit, or because he felt so comfortable sitting here with Charity watching the stars?

"Then I got the letter telling me she was…in the family way. The letter was dated in late December, but I didn't get it until February. I tried to get a leave to go see her then, but I couldn't. Sherman's forces had launched a campaign trying to take control of the railroad, and General Johnston and his troops were sent to help reinforce the area around Dalton."

He gave the memory tentative free rein and was surprised that it didn't hurt as much as it once had.

"In that letter she said she hated the thought of bearing a son. She wanted a daughter, because girls didn't go off to war." His voice dropped off, and they sat in silence. Charity slipped her hand under his arm.

He reached into his inside vest pocket and withdrew his wallet. His fingers found the folded paper tucked under a hidden flap. The creases were so worn the paper nearly fell apart in his hands, but he carefully unfolded it and held it close to the lantern. "This letter caught up with me in early June that year."

Charity leaned forward to examine it. Her voice quavered slightly as she read it. "Dear Dale. You have a son. He was born April eleventh. I have named him Bradley James."

She glanced back at Dale, and the lantern light outlined the puzzlement in her brow. "*You* have a son. Not *we* have a son." She leaned to look at it again. "She didn't even sign it."

Dale drew in a slow, even breath and blew it out, letting it turn to a frosty cloud and dissipate into the night. "No. It's her handwriting, but she didn't sign it." He folded the scrap of paper and slipped it back into his wallet. "All I could think about was getting home to see my son."

Charity's soft voice blended with the murmur of the wind in the pines. "How long—until you…"

Dale stared at one of the pinpoints of light in the distance. "I was wounded at Peachtree Creek. That was in July. You already know that part of the story. It was early September, I think, that an old man with a mule cart took me as far as Mount Yonah. I walked the rest of the way."

"Oh, Dale. Your leg. Walking so far. How did you ever do it?"

The lights in the distance seemed to waver as moisture burned his eyes. "I had to see my son. He was why I didn't give up. Just the thought of holding him in my arms kept me going." He paused and swallowed hard, forcing the tightness in his throat to retreat. "I remember walking down the road that led to Covington Plantation. There was an odor hanging in the air. Stale smoke. The iron gates at the front of the drive were torn from their posts. I went up the drive—you couldn't see the house from the road because of the magnolia trees. When I rounded the bend—"

Charity's fingers tightened around his arm. "You don't have to say any more."

Dale shook his head and patted her hand. "The house was still smoldering. I walked around the ruins looking for some sign that Gwendolyn had gotten my son out. Two of the slaves, the only two who hadn't run off, came out of the bushes when they saw me. They told me when the scavengers came and started looting the place, Gwendolyn took the baby and hid in the root cellar under the kitchen."

Charity released a tiny gasp, and she whispered, "They burned the house." She covered her mouth, but a muffled sob escaped anyway. She leaned her head against his shoulder, and they sat in silence.

Unmeasured minutes passed before Dale trusted himself to speak again. "Charity, I have something else to tell you."

She lifted her head. "What is it?"

He shifted his position and turned so he could look straight into her face. "I'm afraid you're going to be very angry with me, but please know that I didn't want to see you hurt any more than you already are."

"What are you talking about?"

Looking away from her when he said what was on his mind would be easier, but he refused to allow himself comfort if his words inflicted more pain. He held her gaze. "As an officer in the Confederate army, I had access to the military records. I know where the prisoner of war records were kept."

Her expression crumbled, and even in the pale glow of the lantern, he saw her wince. Was she angry or hurt that he'd withheld the information?

"You probably feel that I've betrayed you, but please listen. Because I was there and witnessed what usually happened, I feared that finding out the truth about your father would only increase your pain rather than relieve it."

The lantern light flickered off the tears that clung to her lashes. Her chin quivered. "I still need to know for sure." One tear left a glimmering trail of moisture down her cheek. "And if at all possible, I want to put flowers on his grave. To say good-bye."

Dale didn't bother reminding her most of the flowers had been killed off by the recent frost. Perhaps they could cut some magnolia branches or cedar boughs instead. How he longed to kiss away her tears.

He was about to tell her he knew which office to contact when a tiny movement caught his eye. He jerked his head around to stare hard at the lights from town. But they were no longer down in the valley. These lights—a small cluster of them—moved just below the ridge. Dale grabbed the lantern and extinguished it.

"Dale, what's wrong?"

He jumped to his feet and helped Charity up. "Shh. We need to go. Now."

"But—"

"Don't argue. Just don't let go of my arm. I know every inch of these hills, even in the dark. We'll be back at the boardinghouse before you know it." He bent and groped through the blackness until he found the rifle.

"Come on." He tugged her close to him and steered her in the opposite direction of the moving lights. If it was what—or who—he suspected, they were in grave danger.

Chapter 18

Dale hefted the third crate of grocery items on the Juniper Springs Hotel's order and carried it through the side door to the hotel kitchen. The cook signed the slip, and Dale tipped his hat, anxious to head to his last delivery of the day. He saved Miss Hannah's place for last, hoping to take a few extra minutes to speak to Charity.

The entire time he'd led her down the mountain in the dark last night, he relished holding her hand—just so she wouldn't stumble, of course. He'd prayed with each step that the cluster of torches he'd seen moving toward them was only a figment of his imagination. But when they'd arrived at the boardinghouse and Hannah met them at the door with the news that some of the Klan members had burned three houses out in Crow Town, he sent a prayer of gratitude to heaven's throne for their safe descent through the inky blackness.

He climbed aboard the seat of Clyde's buckboard and

released the brake. The team moved forward with little urging. Steering the horses in the direction of the boardinghouse, he rehearsed his planned speech one more time. The memory of Charity's wounded expression when he'd told her he had knowledge of military records still hovered in his mind. He'd wrestled all night with a possible way to make it up to her. If only he could be sure….

He pulled the buckboard around to the side of the boardinghouse and hoisted the loaded crate in his arms. A tantalizing aroma of something sweet met his nostrils even before he knocked on the back door.

Miss Hannah peeked out the door. "Oh, Dale, come in. Set that inside the pantry. Charity and I were just having coffee. Won't you join us?"

Dale set down the crate and straightened. Charity stood by the stove with the coffeepot in her hand. Was that a blush on her cheeks, or was it a reflection of the heat from the stove?

He pulled off his hat. "Charity." A smile stretched across his face. "I'd love some coffee."

She retrieved another cup from the shelf and poured the steaming brew. When she handed it to him, his fingers overlapped hers for an extra moment, causing a burst of hope to invade his heart. Oh, how he prayed he was doing the right thing.

Hannah cleared her throat, reminding Dale she was in the room. "We heard that Miles arrested Tate last night. Is that true?"

He released Charity's fingers and tore his gaze away from hers. "Yes. Didn't Miles tell you this morning?"

Hannah nudged a plate of fragrant molasses cookies toward him. "He wasn't here this morning. Sometimes he has to stay at the jail all night."

Dale took a warm cookie and bit into its spicy goodness.

"Mmm." He nodded. "I saw Miles this morning. He said he caught Tate and another man last night as they were setting fire to some of the houses over in Crow Town. A few others got away." He turned toward Charity again. "I suspect the torches we saw last night belonged to those reprobates."

A tiny smile graced her lips. "I'm just glad you came up the mountain and found me when you did." She dipped her chin and lifted one shoulder. "I'm also glad we had the chance to talk last night."

Dale shot a quick glance at Miss Hannah, who took the hint.

"I have a few things to do upstairs." She bustled out of the kitchen, leaving Dale standing there begging God to smooth the way for what he wanted to ask Charity. They sat together at Hannah's worktable with their coffee. He slid his chair close enough to reach out and touch her hand.

He drew in a fortifying breath. "Charity, I want to apologize again for not telling you sooner that I had knowledge of military records. Every time you spoke of your father, I could see the pain in your eyes and hear it in your voice." He dropped his gaze, knowing he might hurt her with his words and hating himself for doing so. "At first, before I got to really know you, I tried to justify withholding the information because you're a Yankee. I still harbored such ill will toward anyone from the North, I couldn't bring myself to help you in any way." He forced himself to glance up at her.

Charity quirked an eyebrow at him. "And now?"

Dale ran his finger around the rim of his cup. "My concern isn't for myself any longer. I don't want you to be hurt any more than you already have been."

Her gaze grew intense and determined. "Dale, I have to know." The plea in her voice nearly unraveled him. How could he have thought she wasn't strong enough to handle any possible result from what he was about to suggest?

"I know. That's why I'm asking your permission to wire a man I know in Atlanta. He works in the federal courthouse in the office of records. He may be able to find the information you seek."

She gasped. "Oh, Dale." Her breathy response told him everything he needed to know. "Yes, of course you have my permission."

He reached past their coffee cups and took both her hands. A slight tremble danced through her fingers all the way to his heart.

Charity leaned back away from the small desk and stretched her arms over her head, turning her neck this way and that trying to relieve the kinks. Mr. Peabody expected these articles on his desk in a week. As much as she'd struggled and fought for the words and wasted paper trying to find the right angle for each of the four articles, now she had a grasp of that elusive element, the unique twist she sought.

After two days of barely leaving her room, three articles lay at the corner of the desk, completed. Dear Hannah had slipped in and out bringing coffee or a sandwich, offering encouragement and admonishing her to rest.

Charity stood and walked the four steps to the window and looked out across the peaceful town. Everything looked so normal. People came and went, doing their jobs, running errands, greeting friends and neighbors. On the surface, nothing seemed amiss. But Charity knew better.

Tate Ridley sat in jail, charged with the burning of three houses and the lynching of Henry Jarrell. What kind of hate drove a man to commit such heinous acts? Hannah, whom Charity could hear singing off-key downstairs, had lost both her sons in the awful war that nearly destroyed the country. Dale had once been a wealthy landowner, and the war stripped him of his family, his home, and every material thing. There were still those people who cast distrustful glances Charity's way, simply because she was from the North. One couldn't detect by simply looking at another person, what motivated or strengthened them, nor what fueled their passion, be it love or hate.

She looked at the paper lying on the desk and the muddled fog she'd battled for weeks lifted. A clear picture painted itself in her mind. Why hadn't she caught it before? Pastor Shuford had preached it. God had certainly whispered it to her soul. North or South, Yankee or Rebel, it made no difference. True Reconstruction didn't end at readmitting states to the Union, nor was it limited to the election of a state assembly, ratifying constitutional amendments, or adherence to federal requirements. It was as if God lit the wick of understanding and held up the lamp to shed light into all those dark and wounded places of her spirit. She sat and picked up her pen. She *knew.*

The missing piece of the puzzle had been right there all along.

Her exposé on the Reconstruction could not, *must not,* exclude the emotional and spiritual reconstruction that had to take place if the political Reconstruction was to have any true purpose. Her own battle with resentment and bitterness defined what needed to happen within the heart of every person in the country. She dipped the nib of her pen into the pot of ink and, bent over her desk, began writing as fast as God gave her the words.

Harbored bitterness was as destructive as artillery. Hatred inflicted wounds as grievous as a bullet. Rancor provided a place for those wounds to fester. Animosity took captives and malice spread poison. How could true Reconstruction take place without restoration? Restoration couldn't happen without forgiveness. The only way people could forgive each other was to know God's mercy and forgiveness for themselves.

Charity wrote feverishly, barely taking a few seconds to replenish her pen. The words poured from her soul. Her editor may very well reject her point of view, but it was what God gave her. Finally, she set her pen aside and held up the page. It was done. "Thank You, Lord. Breathe on these words, heavenly Father. Use them to change hearts."

A soft tap on her door drew her attention. Hannah poked her head in. "I'm sorry to disturb you, dear, but Dale is downstairs in the parlor."

Charity rose from her desk and smoothed her skirt. "Tell him I'll be right down." She took a quick peek at her reflection in the small mirror over the washstand and pushed a wayward curl into place. Exiting her room, she forced her feet to maintain a sedate pace down the stairs.

Dale stood when she entered the parlor, and Charity's pulse tapped out an accelerated rhythm. Could he hear it? He tossed his hat on a chair and moved to the settee. "Can we sit down for a few minutes? I hope I'm not disturbing your writing time."

She beamed and sat beside him. "Not at all. I just finished the last article."

"I knew you could do it." His smile warmed her all the way to her toes.

She dipped her head as a rush of heat filled her face. "What brings you over here in the middle of the afternoon?"

The grin that had accompanied his congratulatory words a moment ago faded. Unease traced creases in his brow, and his eyes darkened. He reached for her hand. "I got a reply to my telegram."

Charity's stomach tensed, and her breath caught. She braced herself for the expected answer to her search.

"The man I wired works in the records office, as I told you. He looked up the casualty lists from the battles at New Hope Church and Pickett's Mill, since they were so close to each other and happened almost simultaneously." He paused, his lips in a tight, thin line. "He found your father listed under those wounded and taken prisoner. Major C. H. Galbraith was included with a company of Union soldiers who were being marched to the railroad. Their destination was the prisoner of war camp at Andersonville."

Charity clenched her fists. Such horrible things she'd read about that place. And to think her father—

Dale's voice was quiet and even. "Your father died before they reached the railroad. He was buried somewhere along the roadside in an unmarked grave. I'm sorry, Charity. I know you wanted to pay your respects at his final resting place."

She squeezed her eyes shut against the sharp pain that stabbed her middle. A burning lump formed in her throat, and she slipped her hands up to cover her face. The tears won the battle and escaped down her cheeks. Dale's arms enfolded her against his chest, and he simply held her while she quietly wept.

After several minutes, Dale pulled a handkerchief from his pocket and blotted her face. "I wish it could have been different. I'm truly sorry."

She pulled in as deep a breath as she could manage and sniffed. She didn't know if her grief would ever come to closure, but one thing she knew. Her father loved the Lord. Their separation was temporary. She'd see him in heaven one day.

Dale placed two fingers under her chin. "Are you sure you're all right?"

She forced a smile and nodded. "Thank you for sending that telegram. It wasn't what I wanted to hear, but I think it's what I suspected all along. His final resting place isn't an unmarked grave. He is in the presence of Jesus."

Dale nodded and took her hands, giving her fingers a squeeze. "I'm asking Simon for the day off tomorrow. You're finished with your articles. I'd like to come by and pick you up right after breakfast."

Charity blotted the rest of the dampness from her eyes. "Where are we going?"

He looked straight into her eyes with an expression so tender, she nearly forgot to breathe. He brushed the tops of her fingers with his thumbs.

"It's a secret."

Chapter 19

Charity took a deep breath of the crisp morning air. Light frost still encrusted the grass and rooftops, awaiting the sun's warming rays to melt it away. She snuggled into her shawl and tucked the corners around her arms.

She glanced sideways at Dale as he drove the rented carriage down the lane where the last of the autumn leaves relinquished their hold on the tree branches and drifted lazily earthward. He sat tall and strong and held the reins with easy confidence. As if he could feel her eyes upon him, he slid his gaze to her and winked.

"Why won't you tell me where we're going?" She tried to sound petulant but failed. In truth, she relished the excitement of Dale's planning a surprise.

A boyish grin that made Charity's heart turn over tilted the corners of Dale's mouth.

"Be patient a little longer. We're almost there."

She'd not been down this road before, and the scen-

ery passed like a continuous painted landscape. Even the
stark barrenness of the trees bore its own beauty against
the cornflower blue sky. Through the trees she spied a few
rooftops. She pointed in their direction.

"What is that over there?"

"That's Crow Town."

Ivy, the hotel laundress, had warned her against coming out here, but the reassurance of Dale's company chased
away any apprehension. She scooted a tad closer to him.

"Is that where we're going?"

"No."

She waited for him tell her where they *were* going, and
when he didn't, she blew out an exasperated sigh and leaned
back against the carriage seat. She could have sworn she
heard Dale chuckle.

Wood smoke spiced the air with its pungent aroma as
they rounded a bend in the road. A river came into view,
sunlight sparkling off the water as it tumbled over the rocks.

"What river is that?"

Dale grinned. "Do all journalists ask so many questions?"

Charity cocked an eyebrow at him and planted one hand
on her hip. "It's my job to ask questions. And then I write
about the answers I find." She pursed her lips. "Maybe I'll
write about an obnoxious Southern gentleman who thinks
it's great sport to irritate visiting journalists."

He laughed. "It's the Chestatee River."

Dale snapped the reins and encouraged the horse to pick
up the pace. Less than a half mile down the road, Dale
slowed the carriage. An odd-looking structure loomed just
ahead. It appeared constructed of brick with openings here
and there along the sides. A dome-shaped hole yawned on
one end. At least a dozen men labored at various tasks. Dale
steered the horse up the rutted drive toward the activity.

"Dale, what is this place?"

He pulled the horse to a halt and set the brake. "It's a brick foundry. That structure there is a large kiln where they bake the bricks." He hopped down and strode around the other side. "Come on."

She hadn't planned on a lesson in brick making, but Dale's obvious excitement teased her senses. She took his hand as he solicitously helped her step down. They stood for a moment while Dale scanned the work yard. The workers gave them little notice. He captured her hand and tucked it securely within the crook of his arm.

"This way."

She noticed that he measured his strides to match hers, but what she suddenly realized was the absence of his limp. Had God healed Dale's leg, or had He healed his soul? A smile warmed Charity from the inside.

They walked up to a man holding a clipboard, and Dale addressed him.

"Mr. Burnett."

The man looked up. "Ah, Mr. Covington. Good morning." He shook Dale's hand. "This must be Miss Galbraith."

Dale made the introduction. "Mr. William Burnett. Miss Charity Galbraith."

He tipped his hat. "Miss."

"Mr. Burnett and I spoke yesterday at the sawmill when he stopped in to see if we could give him any scrap wood for the kiln."

Mr. Burnett tucked the clipboard under his arm. "I understand you're here from Pennsylvania."

"Yes, I am." Charity gave him a polite nod. "I write for *Keystone Magazine*. I've just finished a series of articles."

"But Mr. Covington here tells me that's not the only reason for your visit." Mr. Burnett glanced back at Dale and pointed across the yard. "Right over there. The man in the gray overalls unloading the firewood."

Charity looked in the direction Mr. Burnett pointed. A young black man, perhaps twenty-five years of age, dragged pieces of scrap lumber off a wagon and stacked them near the kiln. She clutched Dale's arm and drew in a sharp breath. "Dale, is that who I think it is?"

He placed his hand over hers. "We're about to find out."

Hope sprang up in her heart. *Oh, God, please let it be him.*

The young man looked up as they approached, and Charity gasped. He had his mother's eyes. The hope within her burst into joy.

Dale greeted him. "Good morning. You might not remember me. You worked on the plantation owned by my family for a time. I'm Dale Covington."

The fellow lowered his eyes. "Yes, suh, ah 'members you."

Charity couldn't restrain herself a moment longer. "Wylie?"

He yanked his gaze up, alarm etching his face.

Tears burned Charity's eyes, and her throat tightened. "I'm so glad I found you. Your mother, Essie Carver, is one of my dear friends."

The uneasiness fled from Wylie's expression, and his eyes widened. "My mama is still alive?"

Charity brushed a tear away, and a glorious shiver ran through her. "She is. She lives in Harrisburg, Pennsylvania, and she works as a dressmaker. The greatest desire of her heart is to find you."

Elation spread across Wylie's face. "Oh, praise de Lawd, my mama…my mama is alive and safe."

Delight danced through Charity's midsection. She could hardly wait to take the news back to Essie and watch the expression on the mother's face as Charity told of meeting her son.

Dale stepped forward and pulled out his wallet. "Wylie, I took the liberty of checking into the cost of a train ticket to Harrisburg." He peeled off several bills and folded them. He reached for Wylie's hand and slipped the bills to him as the two men shook hands.

Overwhelmed with Dale's act of compassion and generosity, Charity could barely contain her jubilation.

Wylie shook his head. "Oh, no, suh. I cain't take this."

"Yes, you can." Reassurance rang in Dale's voice. "Please." He enclosed Wylie's hand between both of his. "Miss Galbraith here can give you your mother's address."

Disbelief sagged Wylie's jaw. "I can really go see my mama?" He stared at the money in his hands.

"Anytime you want."

He raised his eyes first to Dale, then to Charity. "How do a man say thank you fo' sump'in' like this?" Moisture shimmered in his eyes. "Seein' my mama again is a dream I made myself fo'get."

Giddiness tickled Charity's middle. "I know how much it will mean to Essie."

Wylie thanked both of them again and again, his voice wobbly. They said their good-byes, and Charity took Dale's arm as they returned to the carriage.

Just as they reached the conveyance, Dale halted abruptly. Charity glanced to see what had caught his attention. A black man leaned on a shovel beside a large trough where they mixed clay soil with straw. The man appeared to be studying them intently. Apprehension snagged Charity's stomach. Why was he staring at them?

Memories stirred in Dale's subconscious and drew him back in time. The face that was forever etched in his mind stood before him. Was he dreaming? Could it be?

Dale slowly released Charity's hand and turned to fully

face the man, who now approached them slowly. The man's face took on an ethereal reflection, and he raised his eyes and his hands heavenward.

"Oh, thank You, sweet Lawd Jesus. I'd been prayin' fo' this day, and You gived it to me. You's the God who answers prayer."

The man's words of praise threw open the floodgates in Dale's heart. He knew that voice. He especially recognized the way the man spoke to Jesus. "It's you. You're the man who saved my life."

"An' yo' be the man I prayed fo' all these here years. I prayed fo' you to live, and I prayed fo' God to let me see you ag'in."

God's mercy and grace rained down. Dale took two strides and embraced the man, clapping him on the back.

When they finally released each other, Dale brushed a hand across his eyes. "All these years, I never forgot the sound of your voice as you prayed. Thank you. Thank you for what you did."

An exuberant smile broke across the man's face. "Ah jus' done what the Lawd whisper in my ear."

Dale pulled out his handkerchief and blew his nose. "I've asked myself a thousand times why you put yourself in danger to save me. I know the answer now. But there is one question I've regretted not asking. What is your name?"

"I be John."

Dale gripped his hand. "Thank you, John, for carrying me, praying for me, for saving my life. You are an incredible man."

"I didn' do nuthin'. Lawd Jesus, He done it all. All the glory go to Him."

They parted with a vow to stay in touch. Dale helped Charity into the carriage and set the horse in motion. He reined in at the entrance to the brick mill to look back. John and Wylie were both waving.

Once they were underway back toward town, Charity slipped her arm through Dale's. "Thank you, Dale. I dreaded going home and telling Essie I'd failed."

Her touch made him ache with the longing to hold her in his arms. "I've been meaning to talk to you about that."

"About what? Telling Essie I couldn't find Wylie?"

"No." He pulled the horse to a halt and turned in his seat. "About going home."

The glow on her face lost a bit of its luster. "Now that the articles are finished and mailed, I suppose I'll be leaving at the end of the week."

The ache in his chest spiked. "Do you have to?"

Confusion etched its mark across her brow. "What do you mean?"

"I mean…" He took both her hands. "You've put in many hours of research since you arrived here, and I'd like your opinion. Do you think a Yankee and Rebel can find love for each other?"

A blush painted her cheeks, and she drew in a soft gasp. An exquisite light brightened her eyes. "No. Not a Yankee and a Rebel. But a man and a woman whose lives have been forever changed by God can."

He cradled her face in both hands and lowered his lips, hovering an inch away from hers. "I love you, Charity Galbraith."

Her breath caressed his face. "And I love you, Dale Covington."

He pressed his lips to hers, and his heart danced.

* * * * *

REQUEST YOUR FREE BOOKS!

2 FREE CHRISTIAN NOVELS
PLUS 2
FREE
MYSTERY GIFTS

HEARTSONG
PRESENTS

YES! Please send me 2 Free Heartsong Presents novels and my 2 FREE mystery gifts (gifts are worth about $10). After receiving them, if I don't wish to receive any more books I can return the shipping statement marked "cancel." If I don't cancel, I will receive 4 brand-new novels every month and be billed just $4.24 per book. That's a savings of 20% off the cover price. It's quite a bargain! Shipping and handling is just 50¢ per book in the U.S.* I understand that accepting the 2 free books and gifts places me under no obligation to buy anything. I can always return a shipment and cancel at any time. Even if I never buy another book, the two free books and gifts are mine to keep forever.

159 HDN FT97

Name	(PLEASE PRINT)

Address	Apt. #

City	State	Zip

Signature (if under 18, a parent or guardian must sign)

Mail to the **Reader Service:**
IN U.S.A.: P.O. Box 1867, Buffalo, NY 14240-1867

Not valid for current subscribers to Heartsong Presents books.

* Terms and prices subject to change without notice. Prices do not include applicable taxes. Sales tax applicable in N.Y. This offer is limited to one order per household. All orders subject to credit approval. Credit or debit balances in a customer's account(s) may be offset by any other outstanding balance owed by or to the customer. Please allow 4 to 6 weeks for delivery. Offer available while quantities last. Offer valid only in the U.S.

HSP12

REQUEST YOUR FREE BOOKS!

2 FREE INSPIRATIONAL NOVELS
PLUS 2
FREE
MYSTERY GIFTS

Love Inspired

YES! Please send me 2 FREE Love Inspired® novels and my 2 FREE mystery gifts (gifts are worth about $10). After receiving them, if I don't wish to receive any more books, I can return the shipping statement marked "cancel." If I don't cancel, I will receive 6 brand-new novels every month and be billed just $4.49 per book in the U.S. or $4.99 per book in Canada. That's a savings of at least 22% off the cover price. It's quite a bargain! Shipping and handling is just 50¢ per book in the U.S. and 75¢ per book in Canada.* I understand that accepting the 2 free books and gifts places me under no obligation to buy anything. I can always return a shipment and cancel at any time. Even if I never buy another book, the two free books and gifts are mine to keep forever.   105/305 IDN FVW5

Name _____ (PLEASE PRINT) _____

Address _____ Apt. #

City _____ State/Prov. _____ Zip/Postal Code

Signature (if under 18, a parent or guardian must sign)

Mail to the **Reader Service:**
IN U.S.A.: P.O. Box 1867, Buffalo, NY 14240-1867
IN CANADA: P.O. Box 609, Fort Erie, Ontario L2A 5X3

**Are you a subscriber to Love Inspired books
and want to receive the larger-print edition?
Call 1-800-873-8635 or visit www.ReaderService.com.**

* Terms and prices subject to change without notice. Prices do not include applicable taxes. Sales tax applicable in N.Y. Canadian residents will be charged applicable taxes. Offer not valid in Quebec. This offer is limited to one order per household. Not valid for current subscribers to Love Inspired books. All orders subject to credit approval. Credit or debit balances in a customer's account(s) may be offset by any other outstanding balance owed by or to the customer. Please allow 4 to 6 weeks for delivery. Offer available while quantities last.

Your Privacy—The Reader Service is committed to protecting your privacy. Our Privacy Policy is available online at www.ReaderService.com or upon request from the Reader Service.

We make a portion of our mailing list available to reputable third parties that offer products we believe may interest you. If you prefer that we not exchange your name with third parties, or if you wish to clarify or modify your communication preferences, please visit us at www.ReaderService.com/consumerchoice or write to us at Reader Service Preference Service, P.O. Box 9062, Buffalo, NY 14269. Include your complete name and address.

LIDIR12

ReaderService.com

Manage your account online!

- Review your order history
- Manage your payments
- Update your address

---

*We've designed
the Reader Service website
just for you.*

Enjoy all the features!

- Reader excerpts from any series
- Respond to mailings and
  special monthly offers
- Discover new series available to you
- Browse the Bonus Bucks catalogue
- Share your feedback

Visit us at:
ReaderService.com